Nico Bech-Myer

A Story from Pullmantown

Nico Bech-Myer

A Story from Pullmantown

ISBN/EAN: 9783743332843

Manufactured in Europe, USA, Canada, Australia, Japa

Cover: Foto ©Andreas Hilbeck / pixelio.de

Manufactured and distributed by brebook publishing software
(www.brebook.com)

Nico Bech-Myer

A Story from Pullmantown

A Story from Pullmantown

By
Nico Bech-Meyer

Illustrated

rles H. Kerr & Co., Publishers, 175 Monroe St., Chicago.

A STORY FROM PULLMANTOWN

BY

NICO BECH-MEYER

ILLUSTRATED WITH SKETCHES BY CAPEL ROWLEY

CHICAGO:
CHARLES H. KERR & COMPANY
175 MONROE STREET
1894

TO THE WAGE-EARNERS OF AMERICA.

"O Lord of life and love in whom I believe—how long, how long?"
Page 54.

A STORY FROM PULLMANTOWN.

It was a quiet afternoon in October, 1893, that
month of repose after fulfilled expectations, that
month in which nature prepares for a health-giv-
ing rest during winter, for a calm concentration of
forces, which are to burst into new life at a coming
spring. Surely October, 1893, would also become
a month of repose to the nations, who had exerted
themselves to their utmost capacity. They had
gathered together what brains had thought and
hands achieved, ever since man first lifted a stone;
they had built from it a world of art and beauty,
of intellect and skill, till they themselves stood
dazed by its splendor.

It had been proved, how mankind had made sun
and air and soil subject to the power of the mind.
Now the nations could go home and rest as masters of the earth.

And especially the people of the Western hem-
isphere, they who had contributed the main share
to this crowning of civilization—if they could not

enjoy a well-deserved rest, it would be against the laws of nature.

As the steeples from the World's Columbian Exposition and the voices from the Congresses arose toward heaven, the spirits of the Pilgrim Fathers congregated above to behold a sight: From the ores of mountains only known to them through the red warriors' tales, their children had taken silver and gold and glittering stones; from these and from night-black coal they had constructed monuments for their own daring and skill; from endless prairies ruled by sun and wind, known to them only by faint breezes whispering eastward, had their children brought the heavy wheat and golden maize and wreathed it amid buffalo horns around machines which had plowed and harvested those prairies.

They had brought it by steam, and they had called for it through thin wires of metal stretching from one end of the country to the other.

And words of fraternity and love, equality and brotherhood of man, rose from men and women. Woman had a temple all her own, with marble and paintings and flowers and silks. And from here, too, an incessant stream of words arose.

Some of the Pilgrim Fathers said: "It is words

from the right and words from the left; it seems to
be words, all of it."

"Don't you see," others said, "that the new-
built city is white?　It is the spirit of light and
love, which makes it shine."

The Eastern nations came and uncovered their
heads, giving thanks for the extended invitation to
witness the splendor of the nation of the future;
when they had seen it and heard many words, they
went home.

After this the heavenly city was to be broken
down, as if it had been put too early into this
world.

But the nation who had built it, needed most
of all to go home and rest by quiet every-day work,
in comfort and peace, gaining strength until great
national achievements might be called for again.

　　　　＊　　　＊　　　＊　　　＊

There was a town in this nation called Pullmantown.　It was known as a place filled with men
and women who spent their life working.　It was
not a place where people came to eat and drink
and lie around, watching other people pushing the
world ahead; nor was it a place where gamblers
and loafers and speculators in other people's weak-
ness or folly came to harvest a crop.

In this town lived a set of men and women who
during fourteen years' work had shown that they
realized their place in the construction of society,
their particular ability, their duties as parents and
citizens.   They knew that will to work is the never-
ceasing wheel which drives mankind toward its
aim; daily experience had taught them that the
existence of all depended upon the working-power
of the individual.   They desired to work with the
best of their strength, and to rest only to be better
fitted for new work.   Therefore this town was
known over the world. If it had not been so before,
it would have become so during the summer of
1893.   People from all parts of the world were
taken to the white city in cars built by those workingmen, and the travelers heard with surprise
about such a town filled with thousands of honest
men and women, people representing the energy
and nerve of mankind, without any drones in their
houses or tramps on their streets.   A great many
deplored that time and opportunity did not allow
them to go and see this place so unique in the
world.

In the evening calm of an October day a train
came running with full speed toward this labor-
city.

With his face pressed against one of the car windows, a little boy was sitting on his knees, watching the cows on the fields through which the train was running. Once in a while he lifted his face to a woman by his side, who smiled into his eager gaze; a tall, commanding figure, with expressive, quickly changing features. The likeness between her and the boy was mostly seen in the dark-blue eyes, which, especially in the boy, attained a depth taking in and possessing those looking into them. His movements in bending back and forth, were quick and graceful as those of a kitten, and his skin so clear that it impressed one with a similar pureness of soul inside the fair form. By his other side was sitting a man—a gentleman, one would say, without stopping to think. One glance at the well-built, somewhat slender figure, told the origin of the grace in the child. The face, turned toward the fields, was restful as were the fields themselves in the waning day. They all three looked as people who came from sun and rest and had become filled with it.

At one of the stopping places a young girl got on—nay, not young; perhaps in age, but not in appearance. She took a seat opposite the little boy. She was dressed in a plain gray summer

suit.   Her hat was gray, so were her eyes, and her
face was colorless.   She did not look attractive,
nor did she by any means appear the contrary.
She did not look worn out through work; rather,
as if care had weighed heavily on her young shoulders. Once noticed, people could not help looking
at her again, wondering where her place in life
might be.

And surely, nobody could help paying attention
to what those lips might have to say.

Her gloveless hands were folded in her lap; slim
and nervous did they look; they were not used to
house-work.

The little boy shouted with delight as the train
passed a cow so closely, that it would have taken
more than the drowsiness of a cow to appear un-
concerned had it been a few inches closer.

She looked at him and smiled, a sweet and sym-
pathetic smile, which went to his mother's heart as
she caught it.

The boy ran to the window at the opposite side,
in hope of seeing new sights. The stranger stroked
his yellow curls as he sat down by her, while he
in turn grasped for the locket on her chain, asking
where she got it.

His mother interfered.

"Please, let him talk," the stranger said, in the low, melodious voice indicating culture of heart; "I love to talk with children, and he is such a sweet boy."

The sweet boy did not need to hear any repetition; he crawled noiselessly as a squirrel on her lap and commenced examining her locket, chain, breastpin, buttons and everything in sight.

His mother again remonstrated.

"Let him amuse himself; he is tired from traveling; has he traveled far?"

"Not very far. But we paid our last visit to the World's Fair this morning, and he may have reason for being tired."

At this moment a newspaper went down, which for a while had covered the face of a man by the door of the car. He looked in the direction of the two who were talking.

As if drawn by his look, the young girl turned her head and met his gaze.

A faint color crept under her skin, as if a stream of life struggled to rise to the surface.

He showed a row of superb teeth.

"I thought I knew that voice; if I had known that, Miss Kean, I should certainly have offered my company this morning."

"Thank you; you know I get along very well alone."

She turned to the boy's mother again. "So you have visited the Fair. Did it meet your expectations?"

"More than that," was the enthusiastic answer. "It was a day-dream of beauty. I shall feel thankful all my life, that I was allowed to live at this time; it seems as if my remaining years all must be hallowed by what this summer has brought to me."

"I am glad to hear you say so. It is a blessing for every one who has had so much benefit from it."

"Did it not make the same impression upon you?"

"In some way. Only—I did not look at it as work accomplished; to me it was a prophecy of a better future, when a 'White City' on the earth no more should stand as a crying contrast to the rest of the world. I have only been able to go there three times"—her listener started up in her seat with surprise—"the last time I was there, unshed tears seemed to choke me, as I bid goodbye; thankfulness, bitterness, hope and despair mingled together, but the lasting impression was;

We have created this, we *must* reach to a time when it no more shall be a terrible contradiction."

The little boy's mother again looked surprised and puzzled. Her husband had turned his face away from the shining fields and looked with interest at the speaker.

Suddenly the paper from the corner seat went down again, and two eyes filled with the force of a determined will were turned to the young lady.

"I agree with you, Miss Kean; it was grand to sublimeness from our part, and it was from their part an exposure of rottenness, unprecedented in the history of nations."

An earnest nod was the answer.

The older lady took her little boy on her lap, utterly unable to comprehend the meaning of this. She would have expressed herself, but the noise from a passing train checked her. She contented herself with looking at him. The words from Longfellow's poem were recalled to her memory:

> "The star of the unconquered will,
> He rises in my breast,
> Serene and resolute and still,
> And calm and self-possessed."

Slowly each word arose before her, as she watched this stranger. He was of her husband's build, but of the dark type, a face full of nerve. She noticed with a certain satisfaction, that though his hair and complexion were fully Southern, his eyes were of a deep blue. There was the touch of an artist over his person and attire, devoid of jewelry and display as it was. It struck her, what perfect repose there was in his way of carrying his head! His words appeared to her as contradictory to his personal appearance.

She turned toward her husband and saw him with a look of intense interest watch the stranger, who now buried himself behind his paper again.

On and on the train went, past fields of milkweed and blue-grass, lying as though they were untouched from eternity; it seemed to widen one's soul to look at them.

Tall chimneys and red buildings had been in view for a while; at last the train slackened its speed. Before them was a city of chimneys, factories and houses.

How beautiful! How peaceful!

Green lawns, hanging willows, birches—oh, the birches from Dakota!

She leaned eagerly out of the window, taking in the sight, looking at her little boy and her husband to see a corresponding joy in their faces.

"Look, what is this, there on the grass?" the boy cried.

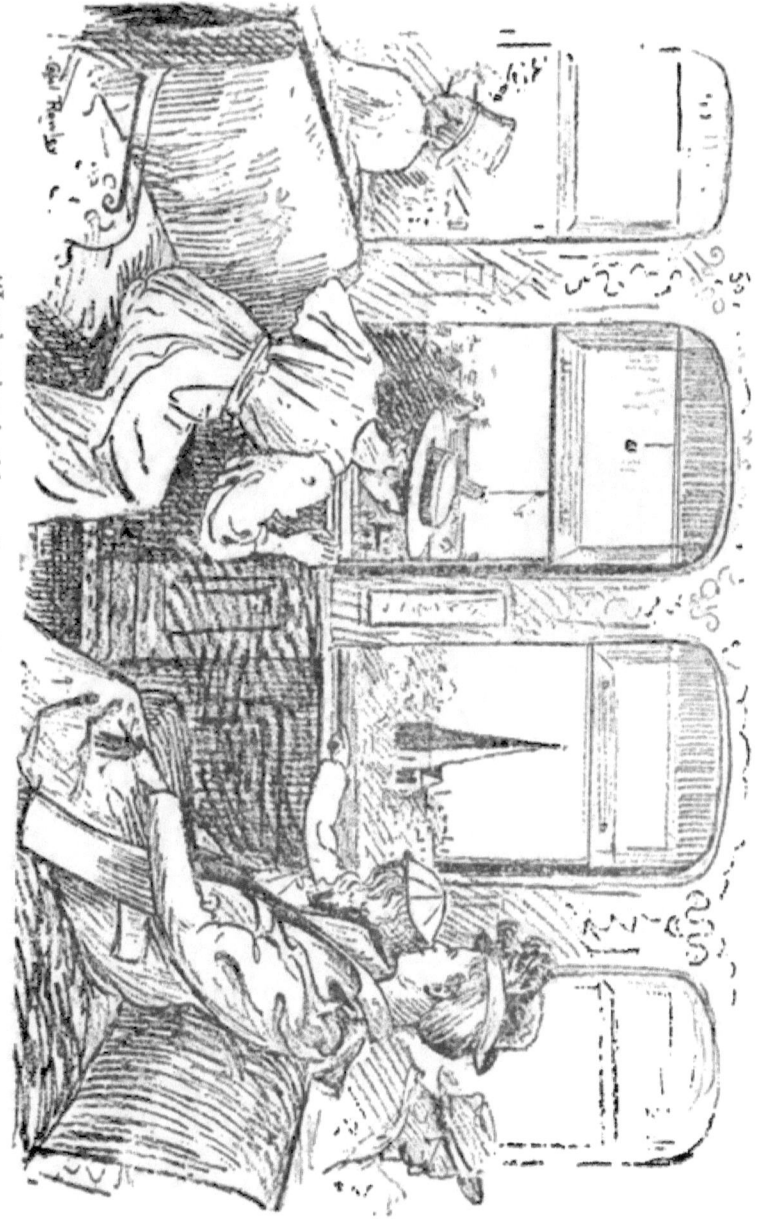

"Look, what is this on the grass?" the boy cried.—Page 14.

"Yes, what is it that is standing there in flowers
—there?"

Her husband followed, where she pointed.

On the slope was standing in pale flowers:

"HOARD."

"That is the name of the owner of this place,
Mr. HOARD."

Flowers, red, yellow and blue, forming beds of
various shapes; hotels and finely constructed
buildings surrounding them.

"What a truly beautiful place!" she exclaimed,
grasping her husband's arm.

"That is what I told you," he answered, with
satisfaction.

At the same moment, she saw the paper in the
corner sink again; a smile, half amused, half pitying, flitted across the face of its reader, while he
looked toward the girl in gray; just the same expression was on her face, and then both involuntarily turned their eyes for a second to the party
by the window.

The train stopped and everybody started to
leave.

"Let me help Earl, and you look after the trunks,"
the mother said.

She was going to step down, but a strange feeling of uneasiness had possessed her; she hardly knew what she was about; a black lace shawl that she had thrown over her arm was hanging down to the floor, and as she was on the step, her little boy was standing in the car on the shawl. He staggered by her pulling it, and the lady in gray grasped him, just as he was going to fall, and lifted him down to his mother. She was profuse in her thanks, as she put on the little fellow's hat and re-arranged his clothes.

"I heard your name was Miss Kean; my name is Mrs. Wright. I hope we will become better acquainted, if you live here. We intend to go into the grocery-business here."

At this moment her husband came with two valises, and took her and their boy along to a hotel. She did not know but she might be mistaken, yet it seemed to her that a meaning glance, pitying, sympathizing, was passed between the two young strangers, who stood side by side, looking at them.

*　　　*　　　*　　　*

Supper-time was past, and the little boy was put to bed, tired after the exertions of the day. Husband and wife were sitting on a bench outside the hotel, enjoying the quietness around them. This did not look much like the working-place it was, at the present hour, where the machinery rested together with the hands that run it. And then, the factories and the houses occupied by the working-people were behind the fashionable part of the place, Mr. Wright said.

The feeling of uneasiness with which Mrs. Wright had been impressed in the car, was wearing off, and what little might be left, she tried to talk away.

"It cannot be any other way, Henry," she said to her husband; "this must be a splendid place for a man in your line of business. A workingman who has work is a good customer; here are no idlers and loafers; they would not be tolerated, as the rent must be paid."

"No, that is true. If only the winter will not be dull."

"There is no fear of that. People here know that their only chance of getting work is with these factories and shops; if they could not get it there, they would leave for some other place, and only those at work would remain. How we shall enjoy getting a home of our own again and to commence doing something! I should not like to travel all my life."

And husband and wife began talking about their

future prospects, while their thoughts all the time turned back to their sleeping child, what they wanted to do for him in time to come.

*   *   *   *

Mr. Wright and his wife had for years lived in a small city in South Dakota. She had been a teacher for many years previous to her marriage, and during the first two years of her marriage, too; but when their child came she gave it up in order to devote herself entirely to him.

Mr. Wright had been a teacher, too, but a delicate nerve-system made him less fit for this occupation, and he became a merchant like his father. At the beginning of the World's Fair and the Congresses they rented out their store and came to Chicago to spend the summer there. Here they met an old friend of Mr. Wright's, who for some years had owned a store in a city of working-people called Pullmantown. Mr. Wright had been aware of the existence of such a place, and that was about all. Their friend's description of this unique place interested them. They had experienced several losses in their business last winter, by having had to trust old neighbors and friends, especially farmers who had suffered through droughts; they were by no means disinclined to change their place of business. This certainly seemed encouraging. Days of hard work in those iron and melting shops would ask for good strengthening food. Steady work strengthens the character of men and makes it safe to do business among them. Their friend could not stand the winters of Illinois, he explained; he desired to go south.

Mr. Wright went out to look at the place. His friend stuck to his side all the time, treated him to a fine dinner in the hotel, took a walk with him in the park, showed him the large tenement blocks and then they took an inventory of the store.

Mr. Wright went back and talked the matter over with his wife and it was settled. They sold their place in Dakota in order to go to Pullmantown.

Mr. Wright had only one objection to what he observed; the rent of the store and of a house such as he considered fit for his family to live in, was exorbitant. He had to pay $50.00 for a store which in Chicago could be had at the rate of $15.00, and $27.00 for a flat which in Chicago before the Fair would rent at $18.00. But his friend pacified him: if business was that much better, what figure would the rent cut?

One thing displeased him even more than the

amount of the rent: no store could be leased here on other conditions than at ten days' notice of vacating. He looked in amazement, nay, with the keenest displeasure, at the face of the renting agent, Mr. Horn, as this gentleman assured him of the impossibility of changing this clause. Mr. Wright was at a loss to understand the cause for such disobliging and tyrannical treatment of renters; but a look at the shrewd, cold face of the business man disgusted him so much that he gave up all attempts of arguing the matter.

He left with only one unpleasant impression of his new place of living—the fact that such a large business center should have their renting attended to in such a way, and through a person who looked more like a piece of machinery than like a human being.

*   *   *   *

On the morning after their arrival at Pullmantown Mrs. Wright went out for a walk with her little boy; her husband being busy in the store and at the depot, arranging things.

It was such a morning in fall as gives back to one all that might be lost in strength during the summer heat. She had intended to get up early enough to see people go to work, but she slept too

She left behind her the better built houses and came to streets and
alleys, where fences were rotting and weeds standing high.—Page 21.

long; the factories had been running for over half
an hour. She passed under the birches out on
the white street—to one side the wide-stretching
fields—wonder who owns all those fields!—to the
other side the city, hammering, snorting, puffing
out volumes of smoke, in its effort to achieve something on this new day.

"My country, 'tis of thee—land of the noble,
free"—it sounded in her thoughts; she did not know
that she was humming it, until she heard her child
keep pace to it.

She left the small park to take a walk along the
common streets of the city. She left behind her
the better built houses and came to streets and
alleys, where fences were rotting and weeds standing high; at many places window-lights were
broken. This made an unpleasant impression
upon her. In the small city where she used to
live, most of the workingmen owned their own
homes, the houses were kept nice and the surroundings made attractive.

She could not help wondering how those places
looked inside. She walked and walked, until both
she and the child became so tired that she had to
sit down on a high sidewalk.

Why in the world was this place laid out that

way? Had men no sense and no thoughts for wom-
en and children? Not as far as eye could reach
had there been a place with trees and grass, where
the mothers, packed together in those prison-like
houses, could go out with their little ones; and yet,
there was plenty of ground all around the city.
Women were sweeping their porches and shaking
their rugs in the neighboring houses; they stood
still and looked down at the strangers. Now men
were walking to and fro in the houses, or rather
to and fro in the different parts of the houses, as
here were whole blocks built in one house, with
families packed together as herrings in barrels.
She thought with a sigh of the cozy cottages in her
old home.

Strange, it seemed as if many men must be out
of work, or what were they doing at home at this
time of the day? Two men came from an alley
and sat down on the corner of the sidewalk. She
liked their appearance, and went to them.

"Will you please tell me, gentlemen, is there
nothing in the way of trees or grass or flowers in
your city, except the small place by the depot?"

"There is a park in the outskirts, where the
train is running. If you wish to see it, we will
show you the way."

They all went along. They passed a piece of swamp-land lying between two of the large factories. The electric car was running between it and the street.

"Why don't they set this out with flowers and trees? As it is, it is unfit for children to play on."

The two men smiled, and looked at each other.

"You seem to be without work," she said, as they went on.

"We have been without work for ten weeks," the tallest of them answered.

Mrs. Wright started back. "What is your occupation?" she asked.

"We are carpenters," the other one said. He was shorter of stature, very dark, with an expression of mirth in his eyes, as he watched the boy bouncing before them. She liked his face, but it seemed as if none of them were much inclined to talk.

At last they stood in view of a park with shrubbery and fine trees, and with bridges across an artificial lake.

"How beautiful!" Mrs. Wright exclaimed.

"Yes. And we have paid for it," the tall man said emphatically. His friend threw a quick glance at him—warning, it seemed to Mrs. Wright.

"But it is too far off," she continued. "I cannot stand it to go there now. Why was it placed there instead of in your midst? You have not in your city a place where your wives or children can sit and rest!"

"I suppose they knew why they placed it there," the tall man answered with a short laugh, and both men again looked meaningly at each other.

At the same moment a train came rushing by; heads were seen through the open windows in the cars, taking in the sight of the park.

As lightning the truth struck Mrs. Wright.

"Oh, I see why!"

"Of course," the two men said and nodded. It seemed as if they were inclined to say more but deemed it better not to.

As they turned to walk back again, Mrs. Wright asked: "Are you Americans?"

She looked at the dark face closest to her, and the answer came with a melodious voice, and a twinkle in the eye, as if he was not sure what effect his answer would have:

"No, Ma'am; I am an Irishman and he is an American."

Mrs. Wright turned her glance to the man towering away over her, and a pair of honest blue eyes met hers; he was so light-complexioned that she would have taken him for a Scandinavian, had not his accent been so pure.

"Are you a Yankee, Sir?"

"If I said so, where I came from, they would shoot me," he laughed. "I was born in Kentucky."

"Well, we may become better acquainted. My husband has bought Mr. Dean's grocery-store, so we have come to stay."

The men looked interested and were about to reply, when Mrs. Wright said:

"It looks to me, as if a great many men all around are without work."

At that moment steps which had been sounding behind them at some distance, came nearer.

"We will let that man pass," the Irishman said to his friend, and the two men made a halt and went each to his side on the sidewalk, leaving a wide space between them; there they stood silently waiting, until a man dressed in a gray suit, like a workingman's Sunday suit, had passed between and walked on.

Mrs. Wright stood a few feet in front of them; the man in gray passed close by her, quickening his speed. His head was bent, his eyes fixed on the ground; a queer, heavy-set, round-shouldered figure it was, like some animal seeking the dust. Mrs. Wright turned around, seeing the two men each on his side of the walk, looking after the disappearing man with a sneer on their faces. As answer to the bewildered astonishment speaking from Mrs. Wright's face, the Irishman said: "There are some people whom you like better to have in front of you than behind you," after which they resumed their walk.

The expression in their faces was so full of disdain, the whole performance so queer, that it dumfounded Mrs. Wright.

"Good morning, Ma'am," the Irishman said, touching his hat, as they came near the street where she had met her escorts.

She walked with her little boy by the hand along the dusty streets, along those immense prison-like structures closing over thousands of human lives, and it suddenly seemed to her as if she was in a city of prisons. Not a yard with flower-beds, not a bit of bright color, not a bay window with a lace curtain, not a balcony nor a cornice, nothing to break the dead lines of those brick walls, which only seemed to lack the iron bars behind the windows. Yet the houses around the depot appeared to be nice enough!

"Nothing to break the dead lines of those brick walls."—Page 26.

Before she came home, she knew that the exterior of this city was constructed on a fraud; now it was left to find out about the interior.

*   *   *   *

It did not take long for Mr. Wright to discover that the "friend" who had sold out to them had not been much of a friend, as the conditions of this place had been grossly misrepresented.

But now they were in it, and they tried to do their best. It hurt them most to realize that they were obliged to sell at much higher prices than those prevailing in the neighboring districts, or they could not make the difference in the rent.

It did not take Mr. Wright long to find out the real truth: that here in this workingman's paradise a great many families were at the border of need.

A grocery-merchant knows without inquiring, in what circumstances his customers are. One pound of sugar and a quarter pound of coffee is enough to mark that family down as being at least very much straitened at the present. Each coming day was a source of new surprise to him; not only that this community was not well off after having for fourteen years been the home of some of the greatest factories in the world, and while streams of gold

had flowed in this direction from all parts of the
United States, but it was as a whole on the border
of need.

*   *   *   *

One bright and cold November afternoon the
Wright family was out for a walk. In front of
them a party of three was walking. Mrs. Wright
knew at the first glance the young man, who sup-
ported a heavy old lady; it was the man from behind the newspaper on the train, and the young
lady was Miss Kean.

Earl bounced toward her, as soon as he knew
her, and a common introduction took place. They
were then informed that the young man's name
was Mr. Wallace, that he was a decorative painter
and boarded with Mrs. Kean.

They all walked together for a while, and Mrs.
Wright immediately fell in love with the old lady,
whose dignified manners betrayed a cultured mind,
and whose white curls spoke about years of experience.

Mrs. Wright insisted on their spending the rest
of the evening together, and the evening dusk found
them all seated in Mr. Wright's parlor.

After supper, as Mrs. Wright came into the parlor, she found Mr. Wallace looking at some illustra-

tions of landscapes from all over the world.   He
showed her a picture from Loch Ness.

"This is from my fatherland."

"Oh, you are a Scotchman!   I thought there
was something strange in your accent.   For how
long a time have you lived in this country?"

"Eight years.   Five of them I have spent in
Pullmantown.   I worked for five years as decora-
tive painter in Edinburgh and for two years in
Paris."

She seated herself by his side and said: "I have
never forgotten you, since I that day on the train
heard you say about the exposition that it was an
exposure of rottenness, unprecedented in the history of nations.   What did you mean by that?"

"It was the skill and brain, the very life-blood
of the workingman exhibited through the agency
of those who trample him under foot.   It was a
wholesale robbery, which could not be punished,
because the thieves were too big.   They set up an
incessant cry about all those wondrous chances
for labor to see and profit by seeing, while it was
a fact that the laborer sat in his home, bitter, despairing, without a cent for car-fare or for admit-
tance fee."

"I   thought   the   laborer   made   so   much

more money in the times previous to the Fair
that——"

"Mrs. Wright, I know of thousands of honest men
and women in Chicago, who never were inside the
gates. And here in Pullmantown, those who did have
plenty of work during the first summer months,
had been without it for so long a time before, that
they were behind everywhere. When the rush of
work ceased, they were either cut down a dollar a
day or they were laid off. You might perhaps
say: Chicago was so overfilled by people from
the whole world, that there exceptional conditions
were reigning. Perhaps, but that was only one
reason more to have the gates thrown open to the
laborers, as all of them ought to see the sights, no
matter from where they came. Now, for instance,
from your city how many came to the World's
Fair? Twenty?"

"No. I don't think twenty came. I should say
ten or fifteen."

"And how many inhabitants?"

"Between 2,000 and 3,000."

"There, you see! Why did not this great nation
declare to itself: the means of transportation shall
be free to every man and woman whose income
does not exceed so and so much; and so shall the
gates of the Fair? Why did not the nation itself

build hotels, the most convenient and cheap, to accept all those who could not afford to be subjected to the greed of private enterprise?"

"That may have been wrong; I have heard several say so. I suppose they did not understand how to arrange it."

"I suppose not. But if they were not able to undertake this task, why was it left to them? Why did we not see laborers as well as capitalists on that committee for the exposition? If laborers had been there, they would have looked out for the interest of the laborers; the money of the capitalist could look out for them. The exhibition was ours; why were we left out from taking charge of it?——Just the same in the Woman's Building. I will tell you what right labor had there. A woman with a good name, but struggling under a condition of combined circumstances, which could not have been helped, and which was near killing her and her family, came to the Woman's Building, asking those women, who had received the hundreds of thousands wherewith to run the women's part of the Fair, for something to do on their premises. She spoke seven languages, she had been a public teacher, she was a practical woman, skilled in housework and handiwork—they,

after many fruitless implorings, offered her a situation in the French department; five hours'
work, dusting show-cases, etc.   Ten dollars a
month as pay."

Mrs. Wright dropped the album and almost cried:
"You must be mistaken!"

"I am not mistaken.   I know her personally.   I
was in her home in Chicago, when she came home
heartbroken and sat down by three little ones and
a husband weak from sickness and unemployed."

"I wonder that the very walls of the Woman's
Building did not tumble down while witnessing
such outrages!"

"I guess they have witnessed more than that,"
he calmly answered.

Mr. Wright, who had been quietly listening from
his rocking-chair, came and took a seat by the
two who were talking.

"I will tell you, what I cannot understand, Mr.
Wallace.   I, as a store-keeper, cannot help knowing the circumstances of this place.   Here are
people who have worked in these factories for ten,
thirteen years; to-day they are without money.
Where has it gone to?   What is the cause of all
this?"

"When you have lived here one year longer, you

will be able to answer all such questions yourself. But it takes time to see into this entangled web. At all other places in the world, people are allowed to buy their home and save the rent. You could not buy a lot in Pullmantown, if you would cover it with gold. For fourteen years the workingman has been obliged to throw exorbitant amounts of rent out of the window and still have no home; while he under just circumstances with his steady work would have paid for his home three times during those years."

Here Miss Kean lifted her head from the photographs of the Fair, at which she and her mother were looking:

"Let me give you an example, Mrs. Wright. I have lived in one house for eleven years, and have paid $17.81 a month; that makes $213.72 a year. This house did not cost over $600.00 to build; thus I have paid for it almost four times."

"This is outrageous. Does then MR. HOARD own every foot of ground here?"

"Every foot; the streets and alleys are his; he can order us out of them, if he pleases. The whole business is constructed on the basis of letting his workingmen pay a hundredfold the value of the swamp-land he bought. And it is not only the

money question; but by being sovereign master of
every foot of ground, he can control all classes of inhabitants, he can hinder anybody's coming here,
who might be opposed to the spirit in which his
business is conducted. Instead of giving a place to a
school, or two places, as needed, he builds a school
and lets the city rent it. His word will have weight
in the choice of principal and teachers—if not his,
then that of his hired outfit or of his friends."

Mr. Wright was silent. He thought of his lease,
subject to ten days' notice.

"Almost eighteen dollars," Mrs. Wright said,
turning to Miss Kean again; "that is a high rent
for you and your mother."

"We never were used to a less convenient house;
there is not even a bathroom."

"No bathroom!" Mrs. Wright exclaimed, with
uplifted hands.

"The place is built upon the principle that the
workingman from the molding and melting shops,
from the brickyards and repair shops, from the dirt
and dust and perspiration, is not the one who needs
a bath on coming home. Such a luxury is for the
agents and bosses and managers of the company,
and for those of the merchants, teachers and doc-
tors who can pay for it," Miss Kean said bitterly.

"Does MR. HOARD furnish medical aid to his employees?"

"Yes; Dr. Hunt is employed by him."

"That is at least one good thing."

"Hm—it is very convenient for such a man to have a doctor paid by himself. There might be cases where an outside physician's assistance might come rather unhandy," Mr. Wallace answered, as Miss Kean kept silent.

It seemed to Mrs. Wright as if Miss Kean, who until now had been flushed from excitement, turned very pale, while her mother suddenly drew her attention to one of the plants in the window.

"But tell me," Mr. Wright said, "why do the men not move away from this place and rent houses in the neighboring districts, where they can get them at reasonable rent or be allowed to buy their own houses with the rent which here is thrown away?"

"They have tried it in large numbers," Mr. Wallace answered. "But those who did move away were laid off on the first occasion. It was not in MR. HOARD'S policy to pay for work which did not allow a certain per cent to go back to his pocket."

"They ought to have gone away by the hundreds,

when they found out that there was not work
enough."

"How could they?   The oldest and best workers
had as a rule through their simple way of living
saved a little money out of the millions they made
for Mr. Hoard; that money was standing in Mr.
Hoard's bank here in Pullmantown.   As long
as it was known that a man had a little in the
bank, it was considered good policy to give him work
off and on, not lay him off entirely, and to give fair
promises about better times, as long as he had a
cent to spend on rent.   And it takes a good deal
of money for a man with a family to break up and
go to a new place."

"The doctor's wife said to me the other day,"
Mrs. Wright interrupted, "that it was very con-
siderate in the company to divide the work among
the people these hard times, to give each one two
or three days' work in the week, so as to be just
to all of them."

"Different views of the same matter," Mr. Wallace coolly said. "By giving each man two or three
days' work, he just makes the rent; that is all
which they are after.   Mr. Hoard gets the value
of all his dirty walls, if the families inside them
starve; that is none of his business."

After her company had left that night, Mrs. Wright was taken with a violent fit of weeping.

*   *   *   *

One cold December day Mrs. Wright was studying how to get her washing done. She had let her girl go, as that kind of business, which they at present were conducting, did not allow the keeping of a girl. Her little boy had a severe cold from walking the long distance to the only school at the place; on account of him, she did not wish the washing done in the house.

When she came down into the store, the tall Kentuckian, with whom she the first day became acquainted, was standing there. She liked him, and usually spent some time in talking with him, when she happened to come while he was in the store.

"Could you, Mr. Johnson, tell me where to look for a woman who would do my washing?" she asked him.

"Go to the barracks, and you will find ten for one. I guess they need it, all of them."

"The barracks! Where is that?"

"It is that tumble-down structure of thin walls and poor timber, near the foundry block. A whole block of it, with families huddled together in two and three rooms."

After dinner Mrs. Wright went out on a search. She found the barracks, and went in through the first door to which she came. Up along the narrow steps she crawled, and rapped at a door. A man opened it, wiping his mouth, as if he had just finished eating. He was a strong, muscular man, with an open face, but he looked very thin.

On a lounge in the room a woman was sitting with a baby on her lap; two little girls ran to her from the table, when they saw the stranger. The man found his hat, bid good-bye and disappeared.

Mrs. Wright could not refrain from scanning the table, as she passed it: sliced cold potatoes, salt, bread, and a drop of black tea left in the cup!

Mrs. Wright felt her heart sink.

This was the dinner of an American workingman!

She seated herself by the side of the woman on the lounge, and tried with tremulous voice to tell her errand and introduce herself.

It was a young woman with a pair of brave brown eyes and a decided voice.

"But I see you have three babies; you are not able to do any washing," Mrs. Wright added, after she had told her errand.

"Yes, let me do it. I can, and I shall do it so as to please you," the young mother said eagerly.

Mrs. Wright felt tears starting to her eyes.

"You must excuse me," she said, pointing to the table, "but I noticed this—is—is it common for you to have such a meal?"

The mother put her baby down on the floor and looked full at the stranger.

"I am not ashamed of our circumstances; it is no fault of ours. I will tell you frankly how we are situated. My husband has been without work for fifteen weeks. Now he got two weeks' work and they wanted the money in the bank for rent. I must be glad if I can give him to eat, what you see there."

"But why did you not refuse to pay the rent? You have got to live."

"If a man refuses to pay his rent, the bank-officials will write on the back of his check: Did not pay the rent. And that man will be laid off inside a few days."

"Oh, what a kitchen floor!" Mrs. Wright said. "How can you ever keep it clean?"

"I cannot. It is made of lumber so soft that you can pick it to pieces."

Mrs. Wright looked at the walls painted a light gray, but now black with dirt.

"What do you pay here?"

"Nine dollars for three rooms.   We have lived here for eighteen months.   Last fall I begged Mr. Horn to have the rooms cleaned, but he refused, though we have paid the rent all the time.   We were forced to pay three dollars for a broken basin, which had been broken maybe ten years before we moved in."

"Why did you submit to it?"

"It was deducted from our check.   Two window panes were broken, when we moved in; the woman next door can prove that.   The agent wanted us to pay for them, too, but I told him, if we should have to do without them while we lived here, we would not pay for them."   She pointed out in the yard.   "There you see my only chemise on the line; I have to go without it while it dries."

"What is your husband's trade?"

"He is a carpenter.   He has to pay for his tools himself.   They are very dear.   If one is broken, there goes almost half a week's pay."

"What nationality are you?"

"Americans; born in Michigan, both of us.   I never knew what poverty was, till I came to this place.   If I wanted ten cents, I could go to the pocket-book.   Now I have to go to a neighbor and run my face for it."

"And those little ones—"Mrs. Wright slowly said, and stroked the baby's hair.

Here the mother broke down; the scornful expression gave way to one of sorrow: "That is the hardest. Such a Christmas I never lived!"

That afternoon Mrs. Wright went to the home of one of the other merchants, Mr. Hill's, and had a talk with his wife. Mrs. Hill told just the same tales. "Our books are filled with bad debts from people who always used to pay their bills, and they are suffering here by the hundreds," she said.

The two ladies talked the situation over. It would not do to go home to a warm room, a steaming tea-kettle and a well-filled table, knowing that all around people were sitting in dirty houses, with half-filled stomachs, little of coal and no prospects whatever. Mrs. Hill did not seem inclined to take any standpoint as to the cause of the suffering; she did not appear capable of rising above the line of charity, but as that seemed the only available help at present, Mrs. Wright was satisfied.

Mrs. Hill was a member of one of the churches, and the two ladies went to see the minister's wife. Here they found one of the teachers from the school, who had come to tell tales of suffering betrayed through her pupils.

The next day a meeting was called at the minister's home, consisting of the wives of the other ministers, the teachers, the wives of the storekeepers, physicians; all the prominent women were there, except the wives of the managers, bank-officials, superintendents, and the other agents of MR. HOARD.

Within a week the ladies of Pullmantown were in correspondence with "The Ladies' Aid Society" in Chicago.

"The Ladies' Aid Society" sent out their officers to examine the conditions, and it was resolved to establish a branch of the society at this place.

Rumors of these proceedings came to the ears of the wife of one of the managers, and information about them was carried to MR. HOARD in his princely mansion in the East.

A short time after, the ladies were informed that it was absolutely against the wish of MR. HOARD to have a society by that name established in Pullmantown. His workingmen were not destitute, and he would not tolerate any such thing as an "Aid Society" on his premises.

The ladies did not give up the work, but they changed the name to "The Ladies' Mission," and after this their doings were tolerated or ignored by higher authorities.

For two months this society kept up seventy families, settling their grocery and meat bills every two weeks. After this the means were partly exhausted, as this winter brought great suffering to all neighboring districts.

At one of the last meetings of the society one of the ladies said: "We cannot wonder at the destitution in our midst, as we see the same all around us."

"I don't think you are right in this view," Mrs. Wright said. "This community is different from any other I know of. No tramps or idlers have come loafing to fill up our streets. Those men have earned the millions of MR. HOARD. If they had had the just part of their earnings, they would have been able to stand three or four years like this. Let them now get some of those millions to live on, until there in some way is effected a change in the present conditions—though we do not believe MR. HOARD'S statements at all, when he claims to be running his business at a loss."

As "The Mission" little by little had to give up its work, the conditions were rapidly turning to the worse.

*   *   *   *

The longer the winter lasted, the colder it became, and thus the suffering increased.

Mrs. Wright was in the habit of taking her little boy to school every morning, to be sure that he would not, child-like, saunter along and get too cold.

Later in the day she went to the store. She could not stay at home; her mind was occupied with her surroundings all the time; and in the store there would be plenty of information from all parts of the town.

It was an exceedingly cold day; the windows were covered with frost, though the big stove was running at its fullest capacity. Several men sat around on barrels and boxes. They were laid off, and came here to talk together and get the news of the day.

An elderly man came in, rubbing his hands. It was Mr. Hart, a German, who worked in the foundry. Mrs. Wright had enjoyed many a conversation with him. His small, light-blue eyes twinkled with the humor which fills the North-German Volkslieder. There was something genuine in his quick manners and concise way of expressing himself, which made one never tired of his company.

To-day he, against the rule, seemed downcast. He stamped his feet and unbuttoned his overcoat, while ordering some butter, cheese and tea.

"Did you get the honey I spoke about?" he reluctantly asked Mr. Wright.

"No. It has not arrived yet."

"I don't think I can take it. I am sorry."

"Never mind, Mr. Hart; I will keep it."

"Are you laid off, Mr. Hart?" Mrs. Wright inquired.

"To-day I am; I hope, though, to commence again soon. But we had a cut of fifteen cents yesterday."

"A cut! I thought you said you had one during the summer."

"So we had, Ma'am. We were cut one dollar in July, and the boss said then that we would not be cut any more."

"How much have you now?"

"$1.60. But it is very hard work, and it is dangerous work, too. I have been burned twice."

"You have! How did that happen?"

"The last time was the worst. I was at work with an ignorant Pole. If there is one drop of water on the skimmer, the melted iron will run all over. He took no care, and poured a stream of iron from my neck down to my ankle."

Mrs. Wright shuddered.

"Yes, it was terrible. I was laid up for about a month."

"Did they pay you any damage?"

"They paid my wages while I was sick; that was all."

"How did your boss seem to feel about cutting your wages?"

"I believe he was sorry, but did not dare to show it. The other boss we had was a fine man, a gentleman. He had been here for eleven years, and he left because he could not stand the cuts in our wages. This one would be kind too, if he was allowed to. I could tell he felt bad, as he came in with the paper yesterday. 'I suppose you have heard of the cut,' he said.

"'I have. That's the way you treat us. You promised the last time that our wages should not come down any more. Then you take advantage of us, when hard winter is on us, and you know we have no way of bettering ourselves.'

"'You know, John, I cannot help it; I have to do as I am instructed,' he said, and I could see the fellow did feel sorry. The hardest on me was to go home and tell my wife about it," the German finished, while he picked up his packages.

That night Mrs. Wright wrote to Mr. Wallace and Miss Kean, and asked them to come to her house to-morrow night if possible.

As the two the next evening sat down together in the parlor Mrs. Wright said: "I wanted to find out from your past experience here, and from your fuller knowledge of the present conditions, can really nothing be done to change this state of affairs? People seem to quietly submit to this existence; if they would stand up as a body——"

Miss Kean and Mr. Wallace looked meaningly at each other; then Mr. Wallace jumped from his seat and leaned against the table in front of Mrs. Wright.

"Is it not strange how different people, without knowing it, can resolve to do the same thing, because the course of events has brought things to a turn which decidedly asks for this one action? Last night I was with one man from the upholstery department and one from the brass shops, and we decided on trying once more to organize the working-people of this place."

Mrs. Wright jumped up too: "That is just what has been in my mind for several days—"

"Pardon me," he said, laying his hand over hers; "I want to tell you first, that at the same moment as I was at work for this, Miss Kean, without knowing my intentions, had three girls from the laundry in her room, talking the same question up with them."

Mrs. Wright turned to Miss Kean, who sat with her hands clasped quietly in her lap, but that faint flush, which made her very skin speak, and that luster in her eyes, which beautified her whole being, were slowly rising.

Mrs. Wright laid her arm around the girl's shoulder and kissed her.

Then she turned to Mr. Wallace again: "I do not wonder at the women, as we women have been so used to having no place in social construction; but you men—why have you remained unorganized during all these years, helpless single individuals, exposed to any kind of treatment?"

"We have tried to organize before this. We have tried it twice. But the bosses had their spies among us, and our efforts were reported to headquarters. The leaders were 'laid off,' not to come back to work again—all except a few. I was one of the few, because they did not wish to spare me. The decorative painters have had their union all the time, and nobody dared to object; they could not do without us. You know our work is almost art. But as soon as we tried to establish unions among the rest, the movement was cut off. They did not dare to forbid the unions, so they did not discharge the leaders. They simply 'laid them off' for ever."

"But they could not 'lay off' all the men."

"No, now you come to the point, if the men had all agreed, they could not so easily have fought us. But you will see, the time has come."

"While I remember it," Miss Kean said, "I warn you to be careful, Mrs. Wright. We are surrounded by spies, and will be still more."

Mrs. Wright nodded; she remembered the man whom the two other men allowed so wide a space for passing between them.

"For instance," Miss Kean went on, "I saw you yesterday talking to Mary Hall in the store; I felt as if I stood on coals, and I could not get you to look at me. She is one of the 'dollar girls,' because she is a friend of the boss's wife, and so is Miss Steele, because she was recommended by one of the other foremen. You cannot be too careful."

"Now let us consider what has to be done," Mr. Wallace said. "Miss Kean will take care of the few girls in the electric department, and she, together with two of the girls in the laundry, will organize those in the laundry department; we can count on them all, with the exception, perhaps, of some of the 'dollar-girls.' I have a man for the upholstery department and for the brass-shops. Then there is a German, a very intelligent fellow; he has studied in Munich and is one of the finest machinists and locksmiths in the country, but he is retired, and regards the American workingman with an approach to contempt; his wages have been cut and re-cut, and he does not stand much. If we could get hold of him, he would take every German on the place, and all those from Switzerland and Austria. But I dare not go to see him, as I feel certain that my steps are watched."

"I will go to him," Mrs. Wright said. "I know him. I had a long talk with him on Heinrich Heine and Ferdinand LaSalle some time ago. He is a declared Socialist. He is eloquent, when it takes him, and has a great deal of feeling, too."

"Well, I will leave him to you, then. Next, we must have somebody for the Scandinavians. We have here both Danes, Swedes and Norwegians. They are slow people, especially the Danes and Norwegians; it is a hard task to get their ear, but if once you have it, you will keep it. They are of a steadfast character. There is a Swede, a tall, gaunt fellow with a face like an eagle's; he used to work in the foundry and was a first-class molder, too. He is especially enraged, as he has been treated with an amount of injustice uncommon even here. But I should not dare to approach him either, for fear of giving us away too early."

"I will take him too," Mrs. Wright declared.

"He lives in the barracks, in the rear, with an old Swedish widow, who keeps boarders. His name is Erik, I think—Erik Swanson."

"I shall find him."

"Now it strikes me," Mr. Wallace exclaimed, "there is an Italian painter, a fine fellow of poetical inclinations; we are on friendly terms. I shall work him up and let him take all the Italians in 'the dens' by the brick-yard in his charge."

"And I know a Pole, who works in the brick-yard," Mrs. Wright said. "He has been laid off for a couple of months, and I gave him a basket of provisions for his children, the last time he was here. He speaks better English than most of his countrymen and has been in this country for many years. I am going to try what he can do among the Poles. Miss Kean, we shall rely entirely on you as far as the girls in the different departments are concerned."

"No, not on me. By no means. I am no speaker at all, and very little of an agitator."

"Your person and your life among them will be the best kind of agitation, as soon as they understand that you are in it," Mr. Wallace said warmly.

"Perhaps. I almost think so myself; but as an organizer I shall rely on Miss Welsh."

"I never yet was exactly posted on your circumstances," Mrs. Wright said. "I only know that you work in the electric department, and I might almost have guessed so. What are your wages?"

"Ninety-one cents a day."

Mrs. Wright started back. "I thought you said once that your rent amounted to $17.81!"

"So it does. When that is paid, there is seven dollars left for my mother and myself for a month's living. We could not exist, if my brother in Colorado, who is a well-to-do engineer, did not send us money."

Mrs. Wright folded her hands before her, unable to speak.

"Miss Kean, may I tell your history?" Mr. Wallace quietly inquired.

She nodded.

He turned to Mrs. Wright. "Eight years ago Miss Kean's father was employed by MR. HOARD as watchman by that gate, which governs the entrance to the shops near the depot. One day a carpenter came with a box of tools under his arm. Mr. Kean asked him for his pass, as it was against the rules to allow anybody to carry tools from the premises without showing a pass. The carpenter answered that he had none. Mr. Kean told him to leave the tools until to-morrow and then get a pass.

"The man became so enraged, that he struck Mr. Kean with the hatchet in the face and felled him to the ground.

"Mr. Kean was in an unconscious condition carried to his home, and it took three weeks before he again got the power of speech. He got up and dragged around, but was never able to work afterward, and died at last from the effects of the blow."

"And MR. HOARD, what did he do?"

"Nothing. The doctor-bill was paid and his wages were paid for two weeks after he was struck."

"Please, Mr. Wallace, don't say so!" Mrs. Wright cried, hardly knowing what she said. "Say that MR. HOARD was never informed of the circumstances!"

"He was. First the widow went to his agents, managers, superintendents, and what all their names are—but they shook their heads; they could do nothing. Then the minister of the church to which Mrs. Kean belongs, wrote twice to MR. HOARD, stating the facts in full and registering the letters, but no answer ever came. Since then Miss Kean has been paying him twice the value of his house, nay, more than that, has practically given him all her time those eight years for the pitiful seven dollars a month."

Mrs. Wright had turned white.

"It is almost a sin to tell you—" here Miss Kean was interrupted by Mrs. Wright slowly stroking her hair.

"Never mind me!" she said; then she glided toward the door and disappeared into the other room.

She walked as in a dream to her bedroom.

Involuntarily she sought the bed, in which her little boy was sleeping; she laid her cheek against his for a moment; then she went to the window.

She raised her hands toward the star-lit sky. "Oh, Lord of life and love, in whom I believe— how long? How long?"

When she after a while returned to the parlor, she saw Mr. Wallace bending over Miss Kean as if supporting her. He moved quickly away on hearing her steps.

Miss Kean arose and went to Mrs. Wright.

"You looked so full of rest and peace, when you came to live in our midst, Mrs. Wright, that it pains me to see how much suffering you have to meet with here. That thought checked me the first evening I was in your house. You remember we spoke of the physician here being an employee of MR. HOARD'S. I came near stating how little a physician knew his true duties, but I felt as if I wanted to spare you. You were happier before you came here."

"I may have been happier in some ways. But I would not have my blindness back again for anything. Let us look truth full in the face and then get up and work."

*　　　*　　　*　　　*

The next forenoon Mrs. Wright went to the barracks. Slowly she ascended the narrow stairway, thinking of how many miserable existences were hidden in this structure, which was erected by selfishness and kept up by greed. She heard voices from the first floor; a man was standing in an open door.

"Well, when will you pay it?" he said sharply.

"Whenever we get work the rent will be paid," an angry voice, apparently a woman's, answered from within.

Mrs. Wright hurried past and up to the second floor. Upon her knocking at the door, it was opened by a tall, lean fellow, who looked as if he had been too loosely jointed together; his trousers were hanging from his hips, and his shoulders were slightly bent.

The narrow, beardless face with the sharp features had a strong resemblance to a bird.

"Is your name Mr. Swanson?"

"Yes, Ma'am."

"I should like to have a moment's talk with you."

He looked suspiciously at her and went ahead of her to a room, looking back, as if he felt uneasy about her presence. A well-kept room it was, bedspread and towels white as snow, pictures, embroideries and quaint vases speaking of a better home far off in the old country. This room must be the widow's room and the best in the house, Mrs. Wright thought. On the floor was a rug of small velvet and plush pieces, such as might be left over in the upholstery department.

He stood and looked at her without offering her any seat; so she sat down on the bed.

"I came to see you about yourself and about the rest of the suffering workingmen here."

His face remained as immobile as if the reddish features were cast in bronze; life was only visible in his eyes, which were fixed on her with a scrutinizing, half suspicious, half astonished look.

"My name is Mrs. Wright, store-keeper Wright's wife."

Immediately his countenance cleared; he came nearer and leaned against the foot of the bed.

He stood and looked at her without offering her any seat; so she
sat down on the bed.—Page 56,

"Oh, I know you now."

"For how long a time have you been without work, Mr. Swanson?"

"I have only had work four weeks during the last year."

"How did you ever manage to live?"

"I sent to Sweden for $300.00 which I had standing there, and when I had lived that up, took out $100.00 that I had standing in MR. HOARD's bank. Now that is lived up too."

"I wonder that you stayed here and lived it up, instead of going somewhere else."

"You see, as long as I had any money they kept on promising me work. So I waited and waited, because I did not like to leave the old lady with whom I am boarding. She has nothing to rely on except what she makes from us three Swedish boys, who are boarding with her. I have bought two lots six miles from Chicago, and have paid $250 on them; now I shall lose them too."

"That is too bad! How did you come to buy them?"

"Our boss talked me into it—myself and several others; I suppose he made a fair commission on them. He kept on telling us to buy them, and we should be sure of steady work. A short time

after, I was laid off, and so were the others in turn.
If I had those $250 now!"

"Mr. Swanson, were you ever in any kind of
union or society?"

"I am in 'The Helping Hand,' a Swedish help-
ing-society. The sick members get five dollars a
week for five weeks; but I have never been sick."

"Where you came from in Sweden, was there
no union in which workingmen could stand as a
body, not only for the sake of sickness and death,
but for the sake of their struggle in life? So that
they all as one man could stand up and ask for
wages which they could live on, and for time
enough to rest in, that they might not be worn out
in their youth?"

He shook his head. "I never knew of any.
They may be there now, but I don't know about
it."

"Don't you think there might be more hope of
bettering your circumstances, if you all stood together as one?"

"I should think so," he slowly answered, as if
struggling to follow the thought.

"We are going to try what can be done, as these
conditions must not continue. We are going to
come together and talk it over, and help each

other.   We want you, too; they say you are a good
worker, and you must be a reliable character, since
you have saved your money.   Will you come to
my home Saturday night?   You will meet friends
there."

He looked hesitatingly up and down at her dress,
her bonnet and gloves.

"You can go to the store; that will be the best.
You know, we must be careful."

He nodded decidedly, as if commencing to comprehend.

"I shall be there, and Ma'am, I have a friend,
a Dane; he knows more about such things than I
do."

"Bring him with you; that is right!"

From there she went to the home of Christian
Dieterle, the German machinist.

She found him at home, as he was laid off for
some days.   His face was lit up with delight, as
he opened the door and knew her.   He ran to the
kitchen door and called his wife, introducing Mrs.
Wright to her.

Soon all three were seated in the parlor, while
two little girls sat in the bedroom playing with
dollies.

Mr. Dieterle was a Bavarian, with the lively feat-

ures and quick movements of the race from this
land of sun and of beautiful scenery. He had
during his youth traveled through all Europe and
was a well-read man. His wife had once been a
beauty, but a care-worn look made her appear older
than he.

Mrs. Wright commenced talking about the condition of labor in the old country compared with
this.

She evidently struck a sore point.

Mr. Dieterle jumped from his chair and paced
the floor.

"The wage-earners in the old country are much
better off than here. I have no regard for the
American workingman——Excuse me, Ma'am,"
as he noticed a pained expression in Mrs. Wright's
face, "I do not wish to hurt your feelings, nor do
I say it lightly. If we in Germany had had your
laws and your institutions to build our work on,
why, we should have had a country of liberty and
equality never yet seen on the earth. Think of what
obstructions the German workingmen have had to
fight against, and look at them to-day: a consol-
idated mass, feeling all as one, educating themselves, incessantly drilling themselves to the fight
which is on, and which never will cease until we

have gained the victory! Imagine us under our
tyrannical government sending Socialists to the
Reichstag!"

"I know you are right. I realize it with humiliation. But remember, you have been suppressed
for so long, but here—"

"That is it! Here they could make a fairly good
living, and with this they contented themselves, like
ignorant children. I have tried time and again to
associate myself with the American workingman,
tried it with honest efforts, but I have no use for
him. And every one who is trained in the old
country labor-school will tell you the same. Why,
take only the Socialistic literature scattered broad-
cast over the country in spite of the government's
vigilance. We are training a new generation in
the study of national economy, teaching them to
take care of their physical self without help from
doctor or druggist, raising them as rational beings,
who do not sell their souls to any church, but
reason for themselves. What are you doing?"

"No. You are right. With us this work is going on in the educated middle class, not among the
laborers. But, Mr. Dieterle, the time is ripe now.
I will not give up my faith in the manhood of the
American laborer. So much has been taking up

their attention in this great, partly uncultivated and partly unorganized country, that they have forgotten to look to themselves as a body; they have prospered individually, until the universal injustice in the construction of society is crushing them too. Now they will listen, and that is what I came to see you about."

Before she left, she saw Mrs. Dieterle with her hands midway on the table, and Mr. Dieterle pacing the room quicker than ever.

They both of them decided to join the meeting at Mr. Wright's house Saturday evening.

*   *   *   *

It was past ten o'clock Saturday evening, as Mr. Wright closed his store after having put the last boxes and baskets in order, and ascended the stairs to his living rooms. As he opened the door, he met a spectacle unusual in their house. Parlor and dining-room were thrown in one, chairs were brought in from bedrooms and kitchen, and every available place was taken up. His wife was standing talking to Miss Welsh from the laundry department. As she turned toward him, he saw that her face was flushed with tears.

And Miss Welsh seemed agitated too.

Men with hard, brown hands and men with fingers like a lady's, figures bent from hard work and quick, intellectual looking men, young girls frail and nervous looking, and older ones fraught with a care which heightened the expression of character in their faces, filled the room. In the middle of it was a woman with snowy white hair, sitting like a grandmother for all. It was Mrs. Kean.

Mr. Wallace was talking with Mr. Dieterle, and Miss Kean had seated herself between the gaunt Swede and his friend the Dane.

Mrs. Wright talked with her husband for a few moments, after which she went to Mr. Wallace.

Mr. Wallace went to the table in the middle of the room.

"Friends! Here we have come together. May it not be in vain! For months men and women at this place have lived from charity. Our fate we have in common with the rest of the world. Those who have the power to take the laws in their hands, have substituted charity for justice. Wherever an organism has outlived itself and is not removed and buried, it decays and poisons the air.

"Thus charity, the dead factor from an outlived society, is to-day filling the world with foulness, and poisoning the life of human beings, who do not get up and remove it.

"Let us begin our work together by denouncing the idea of charity, and when it is wiped out of existence, let us stand on the cleared ground, looking each other in the face, asking each other what is next to be done. I know what I think ought to be done; now I want to know if you think the same. Will any of you tell us what thoughts the last years in Pullmantown may have brought to you?"

From behind the stove the tall Kentuckian arose.

"That is right," Mr. Wallace exclaimed; "we want to hear an American!"

"I am no speaker," Mr. Johnson said, with a slight shaking of his voice; "I only want to say a few words, but they come from my heart.

"We workingmen are in a situation unworthy of men; but in one way it is only just; we reap what we have sowed. We were satisfied as long as we had our three meals a day and a bed to sleep in. If they gave us that, we did not ask what they did with the rest. We left a small minority to make the laws for us and for our children.

"It is hard for a man to get down on the bare

ground; but if that may help him to stand up and beome a man, the price paid is not too high. I am here to-night to say from the carpenters, that they want to organize at any cost. As many as have work say they are willing to run the risk of losing their job, rather than to remain unorganized any longer.

"But we are inexperienced; some of you must come and help us."

There was silence for a while, after he had sat down. Then a fine-looking man who had been leaning against the door-post and with deep interest following every word, made his way through the room. It was Mr. Dieterle, the German machinist.

"I am glad to know that you are an American workingman," he said, heartily shaking the hand of the big Kentuckian.

Then representatives from the molders and upholsterers arose and announced that their men wanted to organize, and those of them who yet had money were willing to pay the expenses.

"I am a man without family," Mr. Wallace said. "I am willing to spend my last cent in behalf of a betterment of the conditions existing here."

Miss Kean looked at him, until her gaze at-

tracted his attention. She then sent him an earnest nod.

"I am with you up to half of my property, if I
then could see you people organized," Mr. Wright
declared.

Mrs. Wright left her place and went to her husband's side.

It was decided to hold another meeting next
Saturday, and then have every one of the factories
and shops represented.

Miss Welsh told about the gross injustice taking
place in the laundry. Girls working side by side,
doing the same work with the same ability, were
paid 80 cents, 91 cents or a dollar, just as it suited
the foreman to put the price. She deplored the
demoralizing effect this way of doing business natu-
rally would have on the girls; still she knew that
a great majority of them would be in for organization.

    *   *   *   *

February had come, with its short, sunless days
and long evenings, those evenings so highly valued
by those who can gather around their books and
papers in warm and cozy rooms.

In Mrs. Wright's parlor the light from the gas
and from the shining windows in the store tried to
make one forget the cold outside.

This room, in contrast with the common American merchant-home, had its walls lined with books. There were only a few pictures on the walls, fine engravings most of them. One of them represented the Aral Sea. Two flamingoes were the only living beings; they were standing in the water surrounded by rushes; around them were sky and water meeting each other, gliding together in a silent embrace; the picture might as well represent eternal rest.

Miss Kean was sitting in one of the rocking-chairs. She was alone in the room. She had been reading, but now her book lay in her lap, and her eyes sought the picture in front of her.

It seemed to pour rest into her soul, and she felt for a moment as if she needed rest, harmony, peace —needed for a moment to leave behind her the struggle and suffering, the bitterness and despair, which usually met her. How good, how grand of character, how wide-seeing and how near the ideal type of man those ought to be who lived in harmonious surroundings! she thought with a sigh. What a race of men and women we would get, if there were houses with marble steps, paintings on the walls, no leaking faucets and plenty of apples upon the table! And most of all, if there was no more any uncertainty about the coming day, if in sickness or old age or death, no matter what might happen, every human being knew that the privilege of a truly human life was theirs!

Sometimes it seemed so hopeless. The worst was not the daily sufferings for the necessity of life; the worst was the waste of strength which might have gone to form a better race.

The intellect, the energy, the true manhood of which she every day saw traces among those workingmen and their wives—to what could it have been developed, had not every passing day done its share to crush it? Poverty ties the soul to the dust. Here was a community where during fourteen years no food for man's intellect had been found. How superior human mind must be, if men can pass through the ordeal of such fourteen years and not entirely lose the stamp of manhood!

A library—such a mockery! A fraud like all the rest! Three dollars a year as a fee from men who needed every penny; and then, what old, antiquated reading did it contain! The rulers of this place took care that nothing which might encourage genuine thinking came within those walls.

Lectures! Once in a while a Republican lecture, which was an insult to these men, who in silence grinded their teeth against it.

And those mothers in the prisons, without nice yards, without gardens, with dusty roads and swamp land around them, with nothing in their homes to impress the children's mind with beauty —during all these years they had been obliged to do without a kindergarten, until the city a few months ago had seen fit to take steps in that direction!

Miss Kean looked again at those walls lined with books and at the peaceful pictures.

"Replenish the earth and subdue it"—were not these the words?

From subduers men had become the subdued, with the exception of a small number.

It seemed to her as if youth never had been hers, as if her years were an hundred.

Steps were heard in the hall-way.

She listened, she lifted her head, and the slow color gave life to her face.

In a moment the door was opened, and a man quickly entered the room.

"You are here already!" Mr. Wallace said, as he greeted her. He laid a package of papers on the table, while she resumed her seat.

She looked in her book; he paced the floor quicker and quicker, looking at her every time he turned.

At last he broke out: "I cannot stand it, Miss Kean; I must speak now, before any one else comes in.   All day have I been promising myself that the first moment I saw you alone, I should ask for an explanation.

"You knew I was waiting for you, when our meeting last night broke up; why would you not let me take you home?"

She looked appealingly at him.

He came to the table close by her chair.

"You must answer me, or it will drive me crazy."

"You know I am always glad to have your company, Mark—but—last night I did not wish for it."

"And why not? I pray, let me know your thoughts; it may be the best for both of us."

She clasped her hands with a pained expression.

"I do not know my thoughts myself; how, then, can I let you know them?"

"Was it because of—because of what I said to you in the hall-way?"

She did not answer, but he saw that her eyes were filled with tears.

"You knew what I was going to tell you on our way home, and you did not wish to hear it. I can only say: even if the time never should come when you might wish to hear it, my feelings toward you will never be changed."

He suddenly understood that this was her original self, the one she would have been, had not the struggle for existence been gnawing her youth.—Page 71.

"I do not want a shadow of a misunderstanding between us; we are friends and shall be so forever —but—if I only could explain myself! Don't you know from your own life, Mark, that there are times of quietness when we feel ourselves mostly as individuals, living our own life, absorbed in our own interest; and again, there are times when our own self is swallowed up, becoming identified with all the souls around us?"

She arose and walked to the opposite side of the table, he looked into her face; never had he seen her look that way before! Her cheeks were burning as he thought they never could; her eyes were shining with a glow which he would have attributed to people of different physical qualities than those belonging to her.

He suddenly understood that this was her original self, the one she would have been, had not the struggle for existence been gnawing her youth.

Overwhelmed, dazed as before a heavenly vision, he remained rooted to the spot, holding her gaze, waiting for further words.

"It is impossible for me to tell you how I have been feeling lately," she went on, catching her breath. "I have been with those people; their suffering has been mine; their bitterness, their hu-

miliation has been mine. It makes no difference
that I have my bread by my brother's generosity,
while they have not; the want of bread is almost
the least; the degradation, the loss of free men's
rights, the utter subjugation under the power of
circumstances!—

"I am a slave together with them; I am degraded
every time they are! Whether it is single individuals that have sold their souls to the devil, as in
the old mediæval tales, whether it is all of us, who
are alike guilty for having built up a society with
slaves and masters—I do not know. I do not
pretend to be able to point at the causes or to give
the remedy; I only see the results as they are.

"There is a time upon us, my friend, when the
life of the individual, personal interests, comfort
and joy, are out of the question, vanishing before
the one all-absorbing question: How can we get
these things adjusted? Do you understand me?"

He nodded. He was unable to speak. She
who had been the personification of calmness, of
patient endurance, she who, according to her own
words, was unable to express herself at liberty—if
all their women were like her, sons and husbands
and brothers would not suffer long!

She continued: "Years ago I promised myself

that I never would bring a child into this life-drain-
ing existence. I had so high a conception of marriage that it seemed impossible to drag it down
into this atmosphere. Wherever soul meets soul,
they ought to enter into life without reluctance or
anxiety, in full joy, in the feeling of their supreme
right to be the makers of their own destiny."

Mr. Wallace would have answered, but at the
same time steps were heard from the kitchen toward the room. He reached out his hand and met
hers across the table. He wrung it silently and
walked across the room to the small table with
plants placed by the window.

Mrs. Wright noticed that Miss Kean was labor-
ing under an excitement unusual to her, but it did
not surprise her; these were unusual times.

The three sat down reading a letter from one of
the leaders of a great labor organization, announc-
ing his intention to come out and remain with them
for a while, in order to organize the workingmen
and call some public meetings.

It was decided to rent a hall in a neighboring
district, as the only one in Pullmantown rented
out at twenty dollars a night, and moreover, they
would never be allowed to hold this kind of meetings in it.

After a while Mr. Wallace prepared to go, as he was expected in the foundry block, where the molders and melters were to meet to-night.

Miss Kean was sitting by Mrs. Wright's desk wrapping up some papers, as he came to bid her good-bye. Behind them Mrs. Wright was busy with her cupboard.

As Mr. Wallace reached out for the papers, he said as answer to the silent gaze which met him: "A new day will be dawning; at that time we shall take up the thread which we dropped to-night;" —and lower—"until then, I thank you for to-night!"

*   *   *   *

During the month of March a remarkable change became noticeable in Pullmantown.

Before this men and women had gone to their work by the twos or threes, depressed and hopeless, uncertain about the coming days and with this uncertainty stamped on their whole being. Half-fed and poorly clad they had trudged along the wonted road to a new day's drudgery, which would allow them a bare existence. Tired from the work they would go home in the evening, dissatisfied with the dirty surroundings and a scant table and without a ray of hope for a better future.

Now they seemed to raise their heads. In the morning eager faces would meet each other; a quick talk, an encouraging word would pass between man and man; they would go to work feeling that a common cause was holding them together. They were no more upholsterers, carpenters, painters, molders, repairers; they were all wage-earners, men with interests in common, a body ready to protect each single member.

Perhaps none of them felt this more than the poor, ignorant Poles and Italians in "the dens" by the brick-yard; these people doing the hardest work, living in hovels built so low that a common sized woman could touch the ceiling with her hand.

Their nationality had always separated them from the other inhabitants of the place belonging to the Anglo-Saxon and Gothic-Germanic race, and so had their work, inferior to skilled labor as it was.

Now they felt that their fellow-men took interest in them; they were not only toilers, they were men with the rest.

The educating effects of organized labor showed themselves from the very beginning.

And as the men among themselves began to recognize their rights of manhood, a hope was growing that it might be recognized by society too.

They came home to supper filled with a new life, dressed themselves and hurried through their evening meal. Those who were not prevented by the care of children took their wives along, and from each prison-like block started a flock of laborers who had commenced breathing the air of freedom—that inner consciousness of human worth of which no tyranny nor deprivation can bereave a man.

Off they went along the swamp land yet bound by frost, in the bitter winter which was prevailing during March, 1894, but above them the star-lit sky and within them the life of a dawning will. They went to a hall belonging to them for those short hours, to meet a friend and organizer who came to help them in becoming men.

The narrowness of their houses, the forced silence under the abuses and injustices of their bosses were forgotten; here was room, and here they could use a free man's privilege to speak out all that was in them. And they were no longer afraid of what they said, since they realized the strength of being a body. They let loose the bitterness of years, their deep-rooted hatred to the man who had bought them, life and soul, their contempt for the miserable creatures of his, who, with a few honest exceptions, had done their share to embitter their lives.

And they did not express their sentiments for their own relief and satisfaction alone; hundreds of sympathizing fellow-men from neighboring districts and from Chicago came to hear their tales.

But it was not alone statements of their degradation—those statements which were bound to come, and to come with a higher degree of violence the longer they had been kept back—which was reported during those evenings. There were declarations of faith, of hope and of love, of faith in justice and truth as the strongest elements, of hope in the dawn of another era for mankind, of love which unites all as one.

The winter of '94—one of the last winters before the great rebuilding of society which now without doubt will come—had brought the majority of the people in the world to a point of starvation. Men and women took the life, which they never had asked for, and which they were not enabled to sustain.

Those meetings of the workingmen from Pullmantown came to many as a voice from above.

Many a suicide was prevented, many a heart-broken man and woman found strength to keep up the struggle by witnessing the self-sacrificing zeal of those workingmen in their efforts to unite. They forgot that they were artists in painting, and unskilled laborers, geniuses in mechanical work, and drudges in the clay of the brick-yard; they only knew that they all were wage-earners, and what money one of them had was the other one's too, until they either starved together or bettered their conditions.

Therefore those evening meetings became meetings of true religion to those who took part in them.

And those from the large city, who came closest to being fellow sufferers with the wage-earners of Pullmantown—the wage-earners in the big stores —came to listen.

Strange how they had the same tales to tell!

From Pullmantown it was told that when Mr. Hoard had given money to a church or to Republican campaigns, his workingmen had had to pay it through a reduction in wages.

From the big stores it was told about two millions given to a museum, while the wages of the employees were put down ten per cent. Thus the employees were forced to give two millions to a museum, while they themselves merely existed, and their chiefs adorned their own heads with a crown of glory for the gift.

One of the sales-ladies from another big store arose and said:

"You know their charity globes from last summer for the babies in Lincoln Park with a: 'Have you put in a dime?'

"They claimed to give ten per cent of their profit for three days of the week to this purpose; how did they dare to give away the money robbed from us, while we were half starving? I used to have seven dollars a week in the glove department; at the same time as they gave away ten per cent of the profit, they paid me four dollars!

"I would see my fingers rot before I would put one cent in their globes."

An uproar of approval arose from haggard-looking citizens to whom public charity had offered soup twice a day for work on the streets, and if they did not wish to ruin their only suit of clothes— those among them who had garments worthy of that name—and thus make impossible every chance of getting work, then they were denounced as tramps and idlers.

One of these men got the floor and said:

"Some years ago a physician in the old country wanted to prove that soup used alone was without nutritious value, but that it, as a stimulant, taxed too highly a system which was not in other ways well supplied.   He put a dog in one pen and gave it nothing but water, and a dog in another pen and gave it nothing but soup.   The last one died four days earlier than the first one.   If this was good soup, what may not be said of city soup?"

An outburst of laughter greeted him in spite of the earnestness of the meeting.

Mr. Dieterle, the German Socialist, asked for a few moments.

"I simply wish to give my definition of the idea, charity.   Those who take upon them to make the laws of our society and to enact those laws have created conditions under which women carry their offspring in anxiety and sorrow, conditions under which babies are born into deprivation of good air and full mother-care; when those babies are near dying, people hurry them to a park and pay for them, rubbing their hands in glee over their own goodness.

"Our rulers make conditions under which men and women are starving, and then they arrange charity-balls, societies and soup to keep back the ebbing life, feeling highly pleased with this their godlike mission on earth.

"Why did they not come forth and pay the millions of taxes, out of which they had cheated the commonwealth?

"Charity is, as a rule, a plaster on a sore conscience. In fewer instances it is a well-meant desire to better society, but a desire taking a wrong aim."

A well-dressed man arose and asked for the floor.

"I am a teacher," he said. "This is the third evening I have listened to you.

"I simply wish to say: You are not aware how many thinking people, teachers, lawyers, physicians, and sometimes ministers too—you have had proof of that yourself"—a cheer from a hundred voices interrupted him, as the people from Pullmantown knew that they had at least one minister in their midst who was a true preacher of life and joy—"how many such people, I say, are siding with you in the position you are taking. You must make your demands, thus showing your valuation of yourselves, and you must make them until they are heard."

Hearty applause followed him, as he withdrew.

*   *   *   *

This time it seemed as if the managers and bosses

gave up their old means of curing the workingmen, whenever organization-ideas beset them; this time nobody was laid off.   The reason was simply that the movement now was so wide-reaching, so determined, that they would have had to lay off most of their force in order to crush it.   But the organized workingmen were abused more than ever by the bosses, especially those who were known as leaders.

The rent was demanded as severely as ever, notwithstanding the unusually hard winter and the lack of work.

Mr. Hart, the German founder, was out of work; and the general depression, in himself, in his family, in all his surroundings, weighed heavier on him inside the walls of the little room.   So he lit his pipe, took down his hat and went out for a walk. It came to his mind, that it was a long time since he was at Mr. Stahl's, a German friend of his, who worked here as a carpenter, and he remembered that Mr. Stahl had been absent from their last meetings.

He went to his house.   He knocked at the door; nobody answered, but as it was standing half-open, he went in.   Nobody seemed to be there.   There was no fire in the stove, and the table gave no signs of any breakfast. He coughed, and slow steps were heard from the bedroom.

A man stood leaning against the door. It was Mr. Stahl.

"For heaven's sake, Mr. Stahl, are you sick?" Mr. Hart cried, and went to him.

"I have been lying down a little—I don't feel well," was the answer, and Mr. Stahl sank down on a chair.

His face turned white, while drops of perspiration showed on his brow in spite of the coldness of the room.

Mr. Hart ran for a drink of water. While he did so, he once more looked at the cold stove, at the clean kitchen utensils hanging on the wall, and the dreadful truth struck him.

He held the water to his friend's lips, and after he had drunk, he moved him to the easy-chair.

"Rest quietly for a moment; I shall soon be with you again," he said, and disappeared.

He ran upstairs to the third floor, where a sister-in-law of his, who worked in the laundry, lived with her old mother. He found the old lady alone at home, hurriedly explained things to her, and soon the coffee-pot was boiling.

"Have you an egg?" he asked.

"No, I have not, but the lady in the rear made a cake yesterday; she may have one."

A few minutes later Mr Hart stood in Mr. Stahl's kitchen with a coffee-pot in one hand, a cream pitcher in the other, bread, a cup with butter and an egg in a bag under his arm.

He placed the things on the table and turned to his friend.

"You need a warm drink, and you must try to eat some; we cannot have you look that way."

Without objections Mr. Stahl was placed by the table, while Mr. Hart waited on him with a half-despairing look in his usually merry eyes.

He did not talk to him during the meal, but after he had finished and looked better, Mr. Hart pushed the things back on the table, took a chair up to the other end of it and said:

"Why do you let things go on that way, Ernst? Why don't you come and let us know how you are fixed? Are we not all in the same boat? Where are your wife and children?"

"I told them to go to her sister's, three miles from here, as soon as they got up this morning. I said I would go to see you later in the forenoon. And so I should have done, if I had not felt too sick."

"For how long have you been situated that way?"

"We have had no fire for three days. The children and Annie have gone out visiting some neighbors, but I was despairing; I thought, just as well lie down and die. To state our circumstances to the boss or to Mr. Hog, the manager, would be of no use, and to live on the rest of you—well, that would only be bringing you down to us too. Still —I should have gone to see you to-day—"

"How long is it since you had any food?"

"To-day is the third day."

Mr. Hart went to the window and stood there for a while, looking out at the streets of this place, where he and his fellow-workers had paid a hundred fold for every foot of ground.

"We have been behind in the rent for the last two months, as I was without work the whole fall; so every pay-day most of my wages went to rent. I have for two weeks gone to work with dry bread and black coffee in my dinner-pail.

"Do you remember the day when Harry O'Shea fainted, while he was carrying iron to the copula, because he had had no breakfast? I was in about the same fix that morning."

*   *   *   *

Mrs. Wright came down into the store after

some coffee, just as Mr. Hart opened the door.

"I would like to have one sack of flour, one pound of tea, fifty cents' worth of sugar and two pounds of butterine."

Mr. Wright put it down on a piece of paper.

Mr. Hart laid a two dollar bill on the counter, and said, while Mr. Wright was changing the money: "Will you please send it to Mr. Stahl, downstairs in the barracks, without saying where it came from?"

Mrs. Wright was there in a moment, and had soon drawn the whole story from the man.

"Mr. Hart, I ask you to let me take care of this. We shall send that family food enough to last for a week at least. And if you would take those two dollars and instead use them for your wife's black dress, I should feel amply rewarded. You know, she has had the goods lying since Christmas, when you gave it to her. The skirt she can make herself; but the waist has to be made by a dressmaker. Will you?"

"I promise you so, and I thank you," he said, while his knotty fingers thrust the precious paper deep down in his vest-pocket.

*   *   *   *

Mr. Hart went to meeting that night with the

intention of bringing up Mr. Stahl's case as the first thing of the evening. But when he arrived there, he found the whole meeting in an uproar over just as bad a case.

Mr. Brown, who used to work in the melting shops and a year ago had one of his eyes injured while at work there, had returned. Though he had spent a year in the East, under the treatment of the best physicians, he nevertheless had lost the sight of that eye. Mr. Hoard had done nothing in the way of supporting him during that year, not even paid his doctor-bills. His boss had promised him work, when he came home, but now he was informed that there was no work.

That night it was decided not to call upon the bosses, agents, managers, superintendents, and what all, any more.

They seemed to have a wide-reaching authority, as long as it concerned the fleecing of the workingmen; but whenever it came to adjusting wrongs or showing human feelings, their authority suddenly dwindled down to nothing.

And they all stuck together in guarding their common interests. After the workingmen had organized, they sent a committee to the head-manager complaining of certain bosses, who were unusually unjust and used abusive language.

The head-manager promised to investigate the matter, but the investigation was limited to inquiring of the bosses about the truth of those complaints.   Their denial was taken against the word of the hundreds of workingmen.

It was rumored that MR. HOARD inside two weeks would make his yearly visit to Pullmantown, and then they would appoint a committee to call on him and present their complaints to him personally.

*   *   *   *

At last a sunny spring-day came, and with the new life bursting all bounds in nature, a new hope dawned in many hopeless hearts.

It was the noon-hour, and the workingmen had taken up their dinner-pails.   Suddenly they were all stirred up by the announcement: "MR. HOARD! MR. HOARD is here!"

Some of them remained indifferently seated with their dinner-pails; others flocked to the doors.

Along the streets a procession was moving. Heading it was a gray-bearded man in a heavy overcoat.   Stout and broad-shouldered, heavy in walk as well as heavy of build, was he. He looked like a log of hardwood compared with the intellectual physiognomies, the nervously pliable statures, and the features stamped with good-will and

Along the streets a procession was moving.—Page 88.

humor of many of those laborers who were looking after him.

Behind him came a trail of followers all his
agents and officials in a line.

Some of them looked a little worried, some
strained; all were trying hard to make the best appearance and have this performance carried out in
the best possible shape.

The girls in the laundry, in the repairing and
upholstery shops, ran to the doors, as the procession in turn passed their places.

Enraged, mocking, laughing, as their disposition
at this moment prompted them, and as especial
injustice or a treatment colored by favoritism called
it forth, they gathered in crowds looking after the
vanishing procession.

"If he does not look exactly like the old hog we
used to have on the farm!" one saucy-looking girl
exclaimed.

"Take care of what you say," one of the girls
warningly said, looking toward the foreman, who
was as busy looking out as they were.

Thus women and men stood looking after that
man, who represented their existence during all
those years—just as they represented his existence,
but in a very different way. A quiet hatred arose

in them as they watched him. Not exactly a hatred against him personally, but a hatred against selfishness, greed and lawlessness; they knew how he and his accomplices of the monopolies and trusts secretly were breaking the laws and gaining their way by throwing other people in the ditch.

*   *   *   *

That night a most determined meeting was held.

Mr. Brown, the man who had lost his eye, took the floor and said:

"The man whose fortune we during fourteen years have made, after he through questionable means had got his patent on a poor man's invention, has been on our premises to-day.   I say 'ours,' for this place is morally speaking, ours; the tools and the shops, and the factories, all of it is ours.

"He ought to be our best friend, to whom we could go in cases of need, in every trouble which befell us.   If he could not live among us personally, his spirit should be ever present with us, manifesting itself in helpfulness, justice, and appreciation of our work, through those whom he saw fit to represent him.

"To him goes the money which we make, and to his agents only that share of it which he allows them; therefore we lay all blame on him.   Why does he pass our streets followed by his tools, instead of going among his workingmen, inquiring, sympathizing, like one man with another?

"He claims he is running things at a loss; if so —but we do not believe him—all right, we have made gold enough for him to enable him to stand considerable loss. But if so, why does he not come to us, talk things over with us, ask our opinions and state his own?

"But he feared that if he had come to talk things over with us, we might have asked him several unpleasant little questions, for instance, if he called that upright doings, that a superfluous force of two hundred men have been kept here all the time, so that they might be on hand in case of a rush. Thus in every instance, small or large, the interest of the employer has been looked after at the expense of the employees.

"Are we nobody, we who have in heat and frost worked to furnish him with mansions, and horses, and money wherewith to buy power and independence?

"It may not be his own fault alone, that he is the man he is. He may be a product of the mistakes of the whole society, of ours and of our fathers'; but we must have something concrete to lay our hands on and make an example of; and he is the one nearest to us.

"We will now seek him personally. He may pass us like a stranger on the streets, but when we go to him in his office and demand an answer, he will have to give it. What kind of an answer it will be, time will show."

Later in the meeting the Kentuckian arose and said:

"MR. HOARD wanted to force us into voting the Republican ticket, but we went Democratic with a majority of two thousand. The next time the whole place will vote the Populist ticket, and if he turned us all out and filled his houses with new men, he would create another lot of Populists."

     *   *   *   *

Two days later a committee of three girls, representing the organized women of Pullmantown, went to see MR. HOARD.

Many of these girls once had a good and quiet home. Several of them had old mothers to support, the struggle for existence having been laid upon their young shoulders after the death of their fathers. Almost all of them were nice and respectable girls; working so steadily and living at this place affording so little of elbow-room, one always knew the life of the other one. But their very respectability made it that much more impossible for them to exist!

Many of them had been used to seeing little services in the home appreciated, and great sacrifices valued at their worth. Now they had to give their young lives to work, without having the gratification of seeing that work appreciated; nay, more, it was considered a matter of mercy that work was given to them.

All of them would have preferred spending the time of their youth some other place than in the steam and heat of the laundry, or in the dust and unwholesome air of the repairing shops. But all had will and business sense enough to have felt satisfied with working, if they thus had been enabled to make an honorable living for themselves and their families.

As it was now, with 80 to 91 cents a day and constant feeling of dependence and humiliation, life was not worth living.

Now they were going to see a man who thought himself infinitely their superior, by his sex, by his social position, by his supposedly higher development of mental faculties; while the truth was, that he was on a moral scale far below theirs.

Filled with silent contempt for him, regretting that he was a being to be considered their equal, they stood before him presenting their complaints and watching the heavy, immobile features, while waiting for an answer, which they knew before they got it.

Pay higher wages? He could get his laundrying done cheaper in Chicago than in Pullmantown; it was only out of consideration for them that the laundry yet was in running order. Cut the rent? Certainly not. He was losing everywhere without cutting any rent!

*   *   *   *

As report was brought to the meeting that night about the failure with which the women's committee had met, it was decided to send a committee of three men to MR. HOARD.

They had little hope of any inclination on his part to listen to them; but they wanted to feel certain that all which could be done, was done. The committee was chosen and the statements drawn and signed by the representatives of each union.

Mr. Wallace, Mr. Johnson, and Mr. Dieterle were chosen for the committee.

It was Saturday evening, and the coming Monday was appointed for calling on MR. HOARD.

Sunday passed very quietly. No meeting was to be held that night; everybody was at home awaiting patiently the turn of events.

A great many went to church in the afternoon to listen to words of comfort from their beloved minister. And they left church strengthened in the hope that it was not only in a far-away hereafter that life was meant to be beautiful and true and good. It was to become so here on this earth, as sure as life means joy in the realization of our being.

The peaceful words and the light of truth which shone from the face of their minister and friend, followed them home; and even those who had been most misgiving felt a ray of hope arise; the man who had their destiny in his hand, might be better than they thought; there might be a spot in his soul open yet for the voices of his fellow-men, and that spot might be touched to-morrow.

Sunday night many people were gathered at Mr. Wright's house.

Most of the delegates from the different unions and several ladies were there.

Very little was spoken about the economical affairs of Pullmantown.

Everybody felt that this question had been so

thoroughly discussed from every possible side, that words now would be wasted.

The action of to-morrow was the only thing left to be done. If that should be without result?— They dared not answer that question and therefore they remained silent.

Stories had been told from Scotland and from Germany, from the icebergs of the Northlands and from the hot winds of Texas.

Those people from all parts of the world were here united in one nation; still the different characteristics of each nation were retained, and this fact served to make them yet more attractive to one another. The solidity of the Scandinavian, the high-mindedness of the Scotchman, the warm-heartedness of the German, the enthusiasm and activity of the Frenchman, and the liberality and elasticity of mind belonging to the American, mingled together and created an evening which, for a while, made those present forget the days which lay before them.

They were talking about the literature of the different countries. A Frenchman and a German, with like eagerness, each claimed their country as taking the lead. The German pointed at Goethe and Schiller.

"I don't care," cried the Frenchman; "they were up in the sky, ours have their feet on the ground, and from there they are reaching upward!"

"You may talk all you want," a deep voice from the window-corner said; "all your literature, English, German, French, has grown out of the old Gothic. Our warrior-tales have created 'die Niebellungenlieder' and the songs of the Troubadours of Gascogne. They have stamped both the Normannic and Anglo-Saxon literature of England; they resound from the pages of Shakespeare."

Every eye was turned to the fair-haired Dane by the window, who hardly ever had been heard to say anything before.

Unheedingly he went on: And the moral views and religious teachings of the old Goths are the same as are found to-day in the hearts of the nations and partly in the churches, too. In fact, what our minister told us to-day, has been said in our language centuries ago, almost in the same words."

The whole gathering jumped to their feet.

"Please, Mr. Hansen, recite some of it for us, if you can."

"After I came home from the sermon, I looked

it up, and I can quote some of the most striking
of it.

"The oldest manuscript which is found written
in the Icelandic tongue, or the "Old-Norse" tongue,
is Volve-spa. (Volve, the fate, an old woman,
who was before everything else—time itself; spa,
that is, to prophesy.)

"It tells about the beginning of this world:

> " 'There was in the dawn
> Of the earliest time
> Neither land nor sea,
> Nor cooling waves;
> Only a yawning,
> Indescribable emptiness. '

"Further, it tells about the life and struggle of
gods and men, and their many troubles in adjusting wrongs and making things meet in harmony.

"At last the end of it all is described:

> " 'See, it is rising—
> The sunken land!
> Green as a spring-time
> It grows from the ocean;
> The eagle is soaring
> 'Way over the mountains,
> Looking for fishes
> In sparkling waters.
>
> Gods are gathering
> On plains of Ida;
> Together they speak

About long-past ages,
The power of Loke,
The deeds of the old times,   `
The songs and the tales.

Happily playing
On sun-filled meadows,
They find under grasses
The treasures of olden;
Their dice of gold,
Once lost and forgotten,
Those which they owned
In days of their childhood.

Harvest shall come
From fields unsown;
Evil shall slowly
Turn into good;
Weak and strong
Together inhabit
Abodes eternal.
Do you understand this?

Then comes the mighty
All-framing Spirit,
He who alone
Has power for judgment;
Peace he shall give.
Discord shall harmonize;
Laws He shall lay,
Which eternally last.' ''

It was very quiet in the room after he had finished.

After a while Mr. Wallace went to the piano and commenced:

"My country, 'tis of thee—"

All joined with a solemnity, as if it was a hymn.
But when he came to the stanza:

"I love my country, thee,
Land of the noble free—"

his voice broke down; he arose, closed the book,
pushed the chair away, and went to the window,
turning his back on the rest of the company.

Mrs. Wright and Miss Kean arose and went into
the other room.

When they came back, the guests prepared to
break up; silently they bid one another good-bye,
each of them filled with forebodings, which they
could not give a definite shape to themselves, much
less express to anybody else.

It was about midnight when Mr. Wright turned
the key in the door, preparing to go to bed. In
the parlor stood his wife, her hand against the
table, looking into the room.

As he entered, she said:

"I do not think, Henry, that MR. HOARD will be
more willing to comply with the requests of the
men than he was with those of the women."

"I have no idea that he will either."

"He will turn them off, as he did the girls, and
what then? It will end with a strike."

"Don't say that!"

"It will; I feel it. It is in the air; it is in the faces of those men. I watched the Kentuckian and Mr. Dieterle to-night, and I said to myself on beholding the quiet determination which more and more is taking possession of them as well as of all the others: It will come to a point, where it will be, 'so far and no farther.' And really, what other hope is there?"

Mr. Wright seemed very much agitated, as he stopped in front of his wife.

"A strike—you don't know what a strike would mean in this case, or you would not talk lightly about it."

"I do not take it lightly," she objected, but he did not hear it.

"It would not be a strike against a single man; it would be a strike against monopolies and corporations, against their interpretations of laws, against our representatives and against the President himself.

"And they would all arise and strike back again. It would be a vain effort, resulting in increased suffering for those who already have suffered enough."

"I do not think that ever a strike was lost, even

if it seemed so.   In this case the indirect result
would be, that the workingmen in Pullmantown
would draw the attention of the world to their
sufferings."

"Ada, when we know that Mr. Hoard pays in
taxes on this manufacturing city the same amount
paid for swamp-land, because he pays each new
assessor a certain sum for being allowed to rob the
commonwealth, can we then expect that the authorities, who allow this, should allow strikers to
gain their cause! It is useless, and worse than that!
Let us go to the polls, throw out the whole com-
bination and get our rights; that is the only way."

"That would be one of the indirect results of the
strike.   The sleeping workingmen would be aroused
from the east to the west of this continent, and
they would go to the ballot and stay there.

"They call me an optimist.   I don't care.

"I do believe in truth and justice being the ruling
powers, when it comes to the point. I believe the
time will come when each home in this country—
yea, in the world, but in this country first—will
be a place of rest and peace, of beauty and of love,
and I believe such a strike would be one of the
means which would hasten the coming of such a
time.   I don't see how you can look at our inno-

She had taken a paper from the table and wrung it in her hands,
while she almost defiantly looked at him.—Page 103.

cent child and not believe that the time must come soon, when such little ones will be born into life in its fullness."

"I believe in it, too; but we cannot force it forth."

"Well—that depends on—" she half laughed— "don't you remember: knock at the doors, and they will be opened—seek, and you will find—? Jacob fought with the Lord—they teach us so about the unseen things, but they are careful not to apply this rule to things which can be seen! Never yet have great changes been effected without birth-pains. There are walls which must be torn down, and old stuff which must be thrown out. I say it is cowardliness in men not to strike under certain circumstances. Better to lie down on the street and die than to live a slave's life and leave it as an inheritance to their children."

She had taken a paper from the table and wrung it in her hands, while she almost defiantly looked at him.

"You may be right; I cannot tell. But promise me one thing, Ada; let us not be the first ones to mention the word 'strike.' I could not bear the responsibility. Promise me!"

"I promise you," she said, more quietly.

To herself she thought, that if a strike should prove necessary, there would be enough to mention it, besides her.

*　　　*　　　*　　　*

.The next day the appointed committee stood before MR. HOARD.

Quietly, hiding his rising displeasure, he received them.

Thus they met—those men representing the thousands of wage-earners, of the best, the most skilled in the world, and this man, whose clothes and jewelry and mansions and horses represented the products of their labor.

They looked upon him as the man who fattened on their toil, and who in them only recognized the toilers.

And he—well, he felt intuitively that they stood before him filled with contempt.

Politely and business-like their requests were set forth; quietly and business-like his answer came; but both parties looked through one another, and the man, in possession of the millions, felt himself shrinking before the earnest gaze of those men representing the real owners of the millions.

They received exactly the same answer as the women.

Wages could not be increased; nor would the rent be cut.   His business would then be run at a loss, he said, and they could not expect that.

In quietness they listened to his answer, while they saw as in a vision rising behind his back millions of gold coins, which they had made and he hoarded away.

They were welcome to inspect the books, he added; there they could convince themselves of what he, at present, was making.

It was supremely indifferent to them what at present was made—they, who knew what had been made; still, they looked at the books as offered them.

They were not experts in book-keeping; so in reality this made them no wiser; the books might be "fixed" for such an inspection, or—what had been whispered—there might be a double set of books.

Anyway, it was out of the question, whether the work of to-day paid or did not pay.

But as they were seated with the books, Mr. Dieterle turned the leaves of his, grew pale and grasped Mr. Wallace by the arm.

Mr. Wallace followed where his finger pointed; a long list of names were written on a sheet—

names of all the leaders of the organization work, of all who ever had spoken at the meetings. Mr. Wallace saw his own name, Mr. Dieterle's, Mr. Johnson's, Mr. Hart's. This was the death-blow of that community for years to come.

Their work was leveled with the earth; they would have to leave behind them the suffering thousands chained to the soil, without any hope of . better conditions during their life-time. Certainly the best protective measures Mr. Hoard could use! In silence they laid down the books. and faced each other.

"Let us ask him, on leaving, if our representing his workingmen will result in our discharge," Mr. Wallace said.

So they did, and were assured that it would not.

At that night's meeting the refusal of their employer was announced to the workingmen.

*   *   *   *

The next day, about noon, Mr. Wright came up into the kitchen.

Mrs. Wright was rolling out cookies, and her little boy was watching her.

She turned and looked at her husband; his face was white.

With an exclamation, she dropped the rolling-pin and ran to him.

"Mr. Wallace, Mr. Dieterle and Mr. Johnson are 'laid off'. The foreman took Mr. Dieterle's place, as they had no one with whom to fill it."

"I knew that would be the result!" she exclaimed —"the beginning of the results! Our 'free' country!" she added bitterly.

"What have you now to say?" she asked him.

"Nothing. Absolutely nothing."

He sank down on a chair and reached for his boy.

The child stood between his father's knees, looking up at him with surprise.

She saw heavy tears fall on the golden curls. She could not cry, her throat seemed filled up.

      *   *   *   *

That night forty-four delegates from the work-ingmen's unions gathered at a meeting.

No one else was admitted.

Mrs. Wright did not go to bed that night. The gas was burning full in the parlor; she sat in the rocking-chair, or she paced the floor. Her husband was in bed, but she heard him tossing sleeplessly.

Toward morning she went to his bed-side.

"I want to tell you what I have seen to-night," she said, talking slowly, as one talks who at the same time sees and describes what is seen.

"I see a country rising, filled with prosperity and blessings. No drouth is killing the crops, for the nation has irrigated all which can be irrigated, and no land which risks drouth is used for agriculture. It is laid out in immense pastures. I see nations mingling together as one, and no restraint is laid on their bringing their products to one another.

"I see the mines and the oil-wells and the stones and the metals belong to society in common, as they did from the beginning.

"And in that world I see no wage-earners. They are all owners of the earth.

"And I see people becoming good, and their children still better."

Here she sank down on the foot of the bed, and as he tried to lift her, he saw that she had fainted.

The next day, about ten o'clock, Mrs. Wright got up after a few hours' sleep. She felt stronger, though her cheeks were flushed with excitement.

As she went into the parlor, she found Mr. Wallace there. She wrung his hands without words;

Line after line o. workingmen passed along the street.—Page 109.

she was unable to speak, and it seemed to be the same way with him.

She went to the cupboard after some dishes, as the door was opened.

Miss Kean came in.

Without a word she went to the chair where Mr. Wallace was sitting. She laid her arm around his neck and kissed him. He took her hands in his and covered his face with them.

Mrs Wright left the two alone and went to the kitchen.

About ten minutes later she heard Mr. Wright storming up the stairway.

"Come!" he said. "Come to the window in the corner room!" And he almost dragged her with him.

Slowly, with uplifted heads, in their working clothes, dinner-pails in hands, line after line of workingmen passed along the street. Another crowd turned the corner, were received with a cheer, and fell in line with the first.

Mrs. Wright heard steps; she turned her head and saw Mr. Wallace and Miss Kean behind them.

His face was lit with a light from above; Miss Kean was struggling with an emotion which lifted her shoulders and took away her breath.

"The strike is on," Mr. Wright quietly said, as if it was something he had expected.

His wife grasped his arm and leaned against him.

He drew her closer to the window, pointed out at the procession of men and said: "If we have to lay down our last cent, we will stay by their side."

FINIS.

WANTED—MEN AND WOMEN

MEN AND WOMEN who believe in human rights, who can see how human rights are now endangered, and who want to do their part in the defense of human rights, are urged to let us know where we can find them.

Our work is the publishing of books of social reform; books like this one that expose acts of oppression and injustice, and books that point to some way for bringing about better social conditions.

We need fifty thousand agents for this book, to bring it before the American people, that the lessons of Pullman may not be forgotten. Hundreds of agents already are earning good pay in the circulation of the book.

If you do not need to make money in this way, circulate the book and give the profit to the Pullman sufferers.

Write us for prices by the dozen, hundred and thousand, and write for our list of other books of reform. We want particularly the address of every reform lecturer in the United States.

CHARLES H. KERR & COMPANY, Publishers,
175 Monroe Street, Chicago.

WOMAN, CHURCH and STATE

A Historical Account of the Status of Woman through the Christian Ages with Reminiscences of the Matriarchate

BY MATILDA JOSLYN GAGE

A few brief extracts from many long reviews and letters:

An earnest and eloquent book.—*Philadelphia Press.*

We have read this book with interest and satisfaction.—*Boston Investigator.*

The book will be especially valuable for study in woman's clubs.—*Woman's Tribune.*

The subject is an important one and has never received the attention it deserves.—*Unity.*

The author is well provided with facts and authorities, and uses them to the best advantage.—*Philadelphia Item.*

You always have something to say worth hearing, and know how to say it.—PROF. ELLIOTT COUES, Washington, D. C.

Mrs. Gage, who has long been known as an able and eloquent advocate of woman's rights, rolls up a heavy score of wrongs against women on the part of the church.—*New Orleans Times-Democrat.*

Your splendid book on woman was duly received. It seems to me the most powerful appeal ever made to women, and will rank among the memorable and classic works of all time.—PROF. J. RODES BUCHANAN, California.

The amount of valuable information lucidly and clearly stated in this volume of 554 pages, is amazing. It is packed with knowledge from beginning to end. No one can possibly regret buying it; it is a valuable addition to the library of any free and truth loving mind.—*The Progressive Thinker,* Chicago.

This is a work of a nature which has long been desired; the book deals not only with church and woman, but as its title reads, with woman, church and state. The work is quite encyclopedic. We cannot well convey an idea of the vast number of facts printed in its pages. It is of interest and use to the student of church history, of woman history and of the history of the state.—*The Truth Seeker.*

It shows much research and learning.—*Advance.*

It is a revelation and ought to be read extensively.—*Kansas Farmer.*

The work cannot fail to command attention among thinkers.—*Chicago Times.*

The author claims that self-development is woman's role, not self-sacrifice.—*Brooklyn Eagle.*

The author is very severe upon the Roman church for its part in the subjection of women.—*San Francisco Chronicle.*

Perhaps the fullest and strongest presentation of the case from the radical woman's standpoint.—*Boston Transcript.*

The subject of these pages is not a pleasant one to contemplate, but the presentation is so bold and direct as to impress us with its sincerity, and the language is expressly clear.—*Review of Reviews.*

To the reader interested in human evolution and whose heart is alive to the need of better conditions for race advancement, this book will open up new vistas for thoughtful contemplation.—LUCINDA B. CHANDLER, in the *Arena.*

In "Woman, Church and State" Matilda Joslyn Gage has formulated a collection of far-reaching historic facts which in themselves are silent arguments for the progressive cause the author so ably champions. The author has woven a personality into her writings that keeps the interest awakened throughout.—*Boston Ideas.*

If this work of Mrs. Gage serves to arouse in women stronger purpose and deeper respect for their sex, if it serves to liberate the minds of women from the bondage of ecclesiastical authority, and the spirit of subordination, it will accomplish the work whereunto it was sent by the noble purpose of its author.—*The World's Advance-Thought,* Portland, Oregon.

Cloth, gilt top, 515 pages, $2.00 postpaid; half leather, $3.00.

Charles H. Kerr & Company, Publishers, 175 Monroe Street, Chicago.

Amber Beads. By Martha Everts Holden ("Amber"). Brief essays on people and things, full of humor and pathos. Paper, 50 cents ; cloth, $1.00.

An Ounce of Prevention, to save America from having a government of the few, by the few and for the few. By Augustus Jacobson. Paper, 50 cents.

Asleep and Awake. By Raymond Russell. A realistic story of Chicago, attacking the double standard of morals. Cloth, $1.00.

Auroraphone, The. By Cyrus Cole. Telegraphic communication established with the planet Saturn. Paper, 25 cents; cloth, 50 cents.

Beginning, The. A novel of the future Chicago as it might be under socialism. Introductory letters by Dr. Thomas, Judge Tuley and others. Paper, 25 cents.

Beyond the Veil. By Alice Williams Brotherton. An allegorical poem of the life to come. Paper, 20 cents.

Blessed be Drudgery. By William C. Gannett. The most popular sermon of the decade. A hundred thousand sold. Paper, 10 cents.

Browning's Women. By Mary E. Burt. Essays on the women portrayed in Robert Browning's poems and dramas. Cloth, $1.00.

Cabin in the Clearing, The, and other poems. By Benjamin S. Parker. A large volume of popular poems. Cloth, $1.50.

Circumstances Beyond Control, or, A Hopeless Case. By Luther H. Bickford. A breezy story turning on hypnotism. Paper, 25 cents.

Comfortings. Compiled by Rev. Judson Fisher. A book of selections suitable for use at funerals or for presentation to those in sorrow. Cloth, $1.00.

El Nuevo Mundo. By Louis James Block. A Columbus memorial poem. Cloth; gilt top, $1.00.

Elsie, a Christmas Story. From the Norwegian of Alexander Kjelland. Translated by Miles Menander Dawson. Cloth, 50 cents.

Essays. By James Vila Blake. Familiar subjects, but masterly treatment. Remarkable for purity of style. Cloth, library style, $1.00.

Evolution. Popular Lectures and Discussions before the Brooklyn Ethical Association. Cloth, $2.00.

Evolution and Christianity. By J. C. F. Grumbine. A study of the relations of modern science and popular religion. Cloth, 30 cents.

Evolution of Immortality, The, or Suggestions of an Individual Immortality, based on our Organic and Life History. By Dr. C. T. Stockwell. Cloth, 60 cents.

Facts and Fictions of Life. By Helen H. Gardener. Essays on live topics by one of the foremost women of the time. Paper, 50 cents; cloth, $1.00.

Faith that Makes Faithful, The. By William C. Gannett and Jenkin Lloyd Jones. New edition from new plates. Paper, 50 cents; cloth, $1.00.

First Steps in Philosophy. By William Mackintire Salter. Discusses the questions: What is Matter? What is Duty? Cloth, $1.00.

Flaming Meteor, The. Poetical works of Will Hubbard Kernan. Unique and remarkable poems by a brilliant though erratic author. Cloth, $1.50.

From Earth's Center. By S. Byron Welcome. A novel picturing a society living under the Single Tax. Paper, 25 cents.

From Over the Border, or Light on the Normal Life of Man. By Benj. G. Smith. A book of prophecies and fancies of the life to come. Cloth, $1.00.

Genius of Galilee, The. By Anson Uriel Hancock. A historical novel of the life and times of Jesus. Paper, 50 cents; cloth, $1.50.

Gospel of Matthew in Greek, The. Edited by Alexander Kerr and Herbert Cushing Tolman. Special vocabulary for beginners. Paper, 50 cents; cloth, $1.00.

History of the Arguments for the Existence of God. By Dr. Aaron Hahn. An important work for students. Paper, 50 cents.

Information for Nurses, in Home and Hospital. By Martin W. Curran. Practical and scientific; not a quack "Home Physician." Cloth, $1.75.

Inquirendo Island. By Hudor Genone. A witty but not irreverent story of a country where the Arithmetic was the Bible. Paper 25 cents; cloth, $1.00.

Jetta: A Story of the South. By Semrick. A delightful little romance for summer reading. Paper, 50 cents.

John Auburntop, Novelist. By Anson Uriel Hancock. A story of a western college boy and college girl. Paper, 50 cents; cloth, $1.25.

Last Tenet Imposed upon the Khan of Tomathoz, The. By Hudor Genone. An instructive story of a non-elect infant. Paper, 25 cents; cloth, $1.25.

Laurel Blossoms, or "My Fortune." Compiled by Della E. Billings. Poetical selections arranged for fortune-telling. Cloth, plain edges, $1.00; gilt edges, $1.50.

Legends from Storyland. By James Vila Blake. Stories, new and old, illustrating how the idea of miracles arises. Cloth, illustrated, 50 cents.

Lessons from the World of Matter and the World of Man. By Theodore Parker. Eloquent passages from unpublished sermons. Paper, 50 cents; cloth, $1.25.

Liberty and Life. By E. P. Powell. Crisp, popular lectures on the evolution theory as related to religion and life. Paper, 50 cents.

Manual Training in Education. By James Vila Blake. A summary of the many good reasons for manual training. Paper, 25 cents.

Modern Love Story, A, which does not end at the altar. By Harriet E. Orcutt. Highly original, widely discussed. Paper, 25 cents; cloth, $1.00.

Money Found. By Thomas E. Hill. Advocates national ownership of banks. Full of information on finance. Paper, 25 cents; cloth, 75 cents; leather, $1.00.

Morals of Christ, The. By Austin Bierbower. A comparison of Christian ethics with contemporaneous systems. Paper, 50 cents; cloth, $1.00.

More than Kin. By James Vila Blake. A delightful book, half story, half essay, all uplifting and refreshing. Cloth, paper side, $1.00.

Natural Religion in Sermons. By James Vila Blake. Cloth, paper label, uniform with the author's other works, $1.00.

People's Party Shot and Shell. By Dr. T. A. Bland. A concise statement of the principles now advocated by the People's Party. Paper, 10 cents.

Poems of James Vila Blake. Remarkable for depth of thought and purity of style. Cloth, paper label, red burnished top, $1.00.

Political Facts. By Thos. E. Hill. A handbook of information for American voters. Paper, 25 cents; cloth, 75 cents; leather, $1.00.

Proofs of Evolution. By Nelson C. Parshall. A popular summary of the proofs from geology, embryology, etc. Cloth, 50 cents.

Pullman Strike, The. By Rev. William H. Carwardine, Pastor of the M. E. Church at Pullman, Ill. Paper, 25 cents.

Pure Souled Liar, A. An anonymous novel, "terse, compact, rapid and intense," scene in a Boston art school. Paper, 30 cents.

Religion and Science as Allies, or Similarities of Physical and Religious Knowledge. By James Thompson Bixby, Ph. D. Cloth, 50 cents; paper, 30 cents.

Right Living. By Susan H. Wixon. Sixty chapters of practical instructions for the young on problems of duty. Cloth, $1.00.

Russian Refugee, The. By Henry R. Wilson. A delightfully entertainin story, full of action and interest. 618 pages. Paper, 50c.

Sailing of King Olaf and Other Poems, The. By Alice Williams Brotherton. Full of melody and variety. Cloth, $1.00.

St. Solifer, with Other Worthies and Unworthies. By James Vila Blake. Story-essays, subtle and entertaining. Paper, 50c; cloth, $1.

Seed Thoughts from Robert Browning. Selected and arranged by Mary E. Burt. Imitation parchment, 25 cents.

Self, The, What Is It? By J. S. Malone. A criticism of the philosophy of materialism. Cloth, $1.00.

Sermons of Religion and Life. By Henry Doty Maxson, with biographical sketch by H. M. Simmons. Cloth, $1.00.

Silhouettes from Life. By Anson Uriel Hancock. Stories of the backwoods and the western prairies. Paper, 25c; cloth, $1.00.

Social Status, The, of European and American Women. By Kate Byam Martin and Ellen M. Henrotin. Paper, 25c; cloth, 50c.

Sociology. Popular Lectures and Discussions before the Brooklyn Ethical Association. Cloth, $2.00.

Study of Primitive Christianity, A. By Lewis G. Janes. A critical and historical work, radical and scholarly. Cloth, $1.25.

Theodore Parker. By Samuel Johnson. A comprehensive sketch of Parker's life and work. Cloth, $1.00.

Un-American Immigration. By Rena Michaels Atchison. Facts regarding the character of recent immigration into the United States. Cloth, $1.25.

Unending Genesis, The. By H. M. Simmons. A simple yet thoroughly scientific story of the creation of the world. Paper, 25 cents.

Washington Brown, Farmer. By LeRoy Armstrong. How the farmers held their wheat and the Board of Trade was beaten. Paper, 50 cents; cloth, $1.00.

Where Brooks Go Softly. By Charles Eugene Banks. Simple poems of nature and life. Paper, 50 cents; cloth, $1.00.

Woman, Church and State. By Matilda Joslyn Gage. An account of the status of woman through the Christian ages. Cloth, $2.00.

New Occasions. A monthly magazine containing a series of lectures delivered before the Brooklyn Ethical Association on "Life and the Conditions of Survival." $1.00 a year; 10 cents a number. The following back numbers can be supplied:

1. Cosmic Evolution as Related to Ethics.—Dr. Lewis G. Janes.
2. Solar Energy.—A. Emerson Palmer.
3. The Atmosphere and Life.—Robert G. Eccles, M. D.
4. Water.—Rossiter W. Raymond, Ph. D.
5. Food as Related to Life and Survival.—Prof. W O. Atwater.
6. The Origin of Structural Variations.—Prof. Edward D. Cope.
7. Locomotion and Its Relation to Survival.—Dr. M. L. Holbrook.
8. Labor as a Factor in Evolution.—David Allyn Gorton.

Any book in this list will be sent prepaid on receipt of price.

Charles H. Kerr & Company, Publishers,
175 Monroe St., Chicago.

Lessons from the World of Matter and the ...World of Man...

By THEODORE PARKER, Selected from notes of unpublished sermons, by Rufus Leighton...

" The reputation of Theodore Parker has never grown dim among those who have heard his voice and looked on his face. But now for years his grave has been green beneath the Italian sun, and the hosts of to-day must depend upon books for their impressions as to one who was nothing less than a grand intellectual force in America not so very long ago. His mantle has perhaps fallen upon worthy shoulders, and his chosen work goes on, but the peculiar sweetness and cordial earnestness of his nature can only be learned by the perusal of his writings and collected and printed addresses.

" A volume of selections from Theodore Parker's unpublished sermons has been published in this city. It makes a veritable book of eloquence, from which one draws inspirations, feeling indebted for every page. Poetic beauty and rugged sense look out by turns from Theodore Parker's sentences, just as from her veil of mosses, ferns, flowers and grasses, the brown face of good Mother Earth at times appears, making us bless beauty and utility in the same breath.

" Gladly will be hailed these fragments, rescued from oblivion. They are helpful, beautiful in themselves; and added to their own intrinsic value is the certainty that they will help to make us realize what manner of man we have had here among us, although most of us have never listened to that persuasive and eloquent voice."—*Chicago Tribune.*

" It has been a great comfort to me often to think that after I have passed away, some of my best things might still be collected from my rough notes and your nice photograph of the winged words. The things I value most are not always such as get printed."—*Theodore Parker to Rufus Leighton.*

One volume of 430 large pages. Price in cloth, gilt top, paper label, with steel engraved portrait, $1.25; in paper, with portrait on cover, 50 cents.

Charles H. Kerr & Co., Publishers, 175 Monroe St., Chicago

DARE YOU READ IT?

Washington Brown, Farmer.

By LEROY ARMSTRONG.

The Story of The Year.

"You dare not publish that story," said a prominent Board-of-Trade man who had examined the manuscript.

"I dare publish it if the people dare read it," said the Author.

It is the Farmers' Gospel.

PRICE—CLOTH, $1.00; PAPER, 50 CENTS.

CHARLES H. KERR & COMPANY, PUBLISHERS, 175 Monroe St., Chicago.